SHADOWED BY DESPAIR

CANDACE ROBINSON

For Amber H. and Donna W.,
Book sisters have no limits!

One

Perin
Present Day

His eyelids attempted to pry open. Darkness… Darkness…
Darkness… Where was he? He was dead. He had to be dead.
Except … he could feel something wrapped around his entire
body, cloaking him, constricting him. With desperation, he
wanted to scream—couldn't scream. He wiggled his fingers.
Dirt.

Who was he?
Think. Think. Think.
Perin.
His name was Perin.

Two

Perin
Ten Years Ago

Ten-year-old Perin tried to fix his best friend's, Rhona's, flowered headpiece. Not his best friend—his sister—his secret sister that only he, his father, and Rhona's mother knew about. It was a secret he desperately wanted to tell. At other times, it was a secret he wanted to keep—a thing that needed to stay hidden because it could affect Rhona. And he was her protector—he chose to be.

He stared down at the broken flowers that his father—Belen—had crushed beneath his boot as if they were nothing, as though no one's feelings mattered but his own. Perin yanked out the white and yellow flowers and, as carefully as he could, inserted new ones.

Rhona had lied to him earlier about where she'd been—what she'd done. But he hadn't known why she would lie about picking flowers. She'd always been honest with him.

The next morning, he decided that he would follow her and find out where she'd been going the past few days—*if* she decided to sneak away once again.

Perin lifted the flowered crown and gave it a once-over. It wasn't perfect, nothing he made was the least bit close to that word, but it looked better than the crushed disaster caused by his father. Biting his lip, he knew he had to hide the headpiece until he could find Rhona and give it to her. He set aside a few books and stashed the crown neatly in a corner, before hiding it behind the tomes.

Placing his hands on his knees after taking a seat back on the stool, Perin let out a huff of air as he stared at his next daily task—a wooden bird. He crossed his legs in front of him and reached for the bird that was almost complete. It still wasn't quite built right, and the wings kept sliding, breaking, or falling off. He wanted the wooden bird to be able to fly, like Rhona's favorite story of a boy named Peter Pan who could cross worlds and do anything. Perin wanted more than anything to be that boy. But stories were just that … stories.

As Perin rotated his shoulder, the skin on his back stretched, and pain radiated all the way down. He let out a small gasp but held back the cry that threatened to come out. The ache was still there from where his father had cut him, and right then, it felt as if a small fire had reignited the agony. Perin's father always gave one strike to his back for Rhona, followed by another for breaking his rules. Rules. Rules. Rules. There were too many that Perin found much too easy to break.

Tears pricked at the corners of his eyes, beading against his long, thick lashes. Perin brought his tight fist down on his desk—he needed to stop this. No one saw him tear up because he didn't do that anymore. Rhona used to see him cry when he couldn't make things right, but today it would end. However, Belen had never seen him cry, not once. No matter how hurt he was from his father's words or cuts. Swiping the tears away, he stared back down at his gadget.

"Well, bird," Perin said, "today is the day we're going to get these wings right, and you're going to fly away. You're going to do the things that Rhona and I won't ever be able to do."

He quirked his head and pretended to listen to the words that would never escape the beak of a pretend bird.

"What is that you say, bird?" He frowned and swept the lock of hair from his brow. "I'm an idiot? I know I am."

With his metal pincers, Perin twisted the blue wing, pushing the tip farther in. Holding the bird up, his lips twitched for a moment. He wound up the top in four rotations and tossed the gadget through the air. The wings flapped, and Perin's eyes lit up, yet only for a moment before the bird came crashing to the ground. The gadget wasn't quite there, but it was getting better. Right as he scooped the bird up, the thick fabric—separating his area from the other rooms of the tent—lifted.

Perin's head jerked up, and his heart got stuck in his throat as his gaze landed on the person who'd entered, now standing in front of him. *Belen.*

Before Perin could get a word out, least of all a breath, his father's eyes locked onto the object in his hand. "What are you doing, boy?"

Perin wanted to hide the wooden bird behind his back, but he knew every single time he'd done that, Belen made sure his things were ruined beyond fixing. So he inhaled steadily and stood straight, still nowhere near as tall as Belen's size. "Nothing, Father."

"*Nothing?*" Belen's tone was soft, yet the word fell harshly from his tongue, and his eyes flickered with intensity.

"Well, no, not nothing." Perin avoided staring down at his hand because he wanted to appear on the same level as Belen. Not frightened, because he wasn't that—he was more tired than anything. Perin was already growing taller. Soon he hoped he would be able to hover over his father.

Without peering down, Belen took a step forward and swiped the bird from Perin's grasp. It clattered to the ground with a soft *clack-clack*. And just as Belen had done with Rhona's headpiece, his boot came up, then down, squashing Perin's sweat and tears in one single motion, the sound echoing through the room.

Perin tried to call up anger to the surface to disguise all of his emotions, and it did come—but so did the tears he desperately wanted to keep away.

"What is that in your eyes, boy?" Belen curled his lips into a smirk. "You're so weak—no matter how hard you try not to be."

Perin wasn't weak. The tears dried up, and Perin lunged for his father. Before his hands could shove Belen, his body was thrown in the opposite direction by an invisible force, his back smacking against the feathered mattress.

"Nothing you do will ever harm me." His father smiled. "But you can still try if you really want to. For that disobedient act, you will need to lift your shirt."

Perin didn't move.

"Now." Belen gritted his teeth. "Or I'll crush more things—like I did your miserable bird and Rhona's flowers."

Clenching his jaw, Perin obeyed and turned around, drawing up his shirt. He would take the marks every single time, because if not, Rhona would have to suffer much worse.

Perin closed his eyes and thought about what he would wish for if given the chance. His sister yearned to dance and be happy. He knew he wanted those things for her, but he couldn't think of anything that he wanted for himself anymore. Nothing at all. Because no matter what, he would never be able to fly like the fictional boy from the stories.

Perin stayed in his room for the rest of the afternoon until Belen came back later.

"I'm sending you away for a couple of weeks," his father said. "You will tell everyone you're going on a journey to become a man, but really you're going to go search for the

Stone of Desire."

Perin's brows lowered because he'd heard about the Stone of Desire. Thea, Rhona's mother, used to tell them the story of an alabaster stone who had answered the savior's—Luca's—desire from a dying Earth. She'd even told him how to get there before, but he thought the Stone didn't answer to humans anymore.

"I don't understand."

Belen ran a hand down his low curly ponytail, no emotion showing on his face. "You're going to see if the Stone will wake for you."

"And if it doesn't?" Perin knew it probably wouldn't, but what if it did? Maybe he did have a single wish he could ask that had a possibility of coming true after all. But he couldn't get his hopes up—not yet.

"Then I have one other option." Belen paused, then shook his head. "But it will be a long while for that—Rhona isn't ready yet."

Ready for what?

"And do not mention any of this to Rhona," Belen threatened.

Perin nodded, pretending to be the perfect son as Belen relayed to him exactly what to do. It was a mask of obedience, one that he would have to wear until he discovered what he really wished for, besides Rhona being happy.

He thought again of Luca's story, the one Thea used to tell him and his sister. Rhona loved the story and everything about it. But Perin hated the tale. If Luca was supposed to take everyone to a better world, then why did Rhona have to suffer? Why wasn't humankind kinder, and why wasn't his father better to his own children?

✦⸻

Early the next morning, Perin packed the necessities for the journey in his bag and placed Rhona's headpiece under his tunic. His upper back continued to throb as he straightened, but he pushed the soreness and pain away as best he could. When he reached the Stone, he would have the perfect plan, and for now, that was where his focus lingered.

Outside, Perin found that everyone was still most likely fast asleep underneath the bright pink sky as the twin suns' light filtered in. Without whistling to let his presence be known to Rhona, he lifted the flap of the tent and walked inside her home to where her room rested in the front.

His sister still lay fast asleep, her springy blonde curls surrounding her heart-shaped face. Furrowing his brow, he peered down at her hand and found something clasped there. Multiple small flutes tied together.

He reached to pull the object from her grasp so he could inspect it. Where had she gotten that? He knew she didn't play music or have the skills to make something so detailed. Before his fingers connected with the instrument, Rhona rolled to her back. He snatched his hand away just as she opened her blue eyes. Blue eyes like his—like Belen's.

Her gaze widened in surprise as she jerked forward, sneaking her hand beneath the blanket. When she pulled it from underneath the covers, her palm was empty. Perin didn't ask why she was hiding the flute or where it had come from. It was her secret, and if she wanted to share it with him, she would.

"You're up early." Rhona yawned with a wide smile, shifting out from the blanket.

"Sorry, I didn't come out last night to play. I was tired," he lied—his back had hurt too much. "I do have some news, though. Belen's sending me off for two weeks."

"*Two weeks?*" Rhona slapped her knees as she brought herself to stand. "Why?"

"Oh, just because it's time for me to become a man." He

rolled his eyes.

"That doesn't even sound safe," she said. "I'll go with you. I can wake Mama right now."

He grasped her shoulders just as she was starting to turn to find Thea. "No, this is my adventure, and we'll have plenty together. I promise."

Her chin dropped to her chest, and she gritted her teeth. "I hate him."

"I know." He hated him, too. More than she would ever know. "But you'll be okay while I'm gone." Belen had sworn that to him, and as long as Perin followed the rules, he knew it would be true.

From underneath his shirt, Perin pulled out the flowered headpiece and placed it into her hands. "I know it's not perfect, but I fixed it as best I could."

Rhona's eyes lit up as she took the crown and wrapped her thin arms around him—he tried not to flinch away from her. It wasn't just the pain that was affecting him, but also the touch. It reminded him how the one person who touched him the most always hurt him. Yet she wasn't Belen. He finally relaxed into her, hugging her back, because he trusted her.

After a goodbye and leaving Rhona's tent, Perin stopped at the edge of the forest. There was one last thing he needed to do before departing. He set his things beside a wide tree with only the real sword—that Belen had finally given to him—attached at his hip.

Perin heard the crunching of soft boots against the grass. He snapped back behind the tree, peeking his head out just a little. Rhona tiptoed past a few tents with her snowy-white hood drawn over her head, catching his attention.

The sly little fox.

He was bigger than her, but he knew how to stay quiet as he followed. She scurried around trees with sapphire leaves— once she got past them and farther away from the village, she started skipping.

Perin wasn't going to skip to keep up the pace with her. Instead, he leaped every so often, making sure not to catch twigs or leaves. He passed more colorful foliage, and trees filled with bright green pears, the two suns rising higher and higher.

Where is she going? How far is she going?

The answer came soon enough as the sounds of the river echoed in his ears when he neared. But that wasn't the only noise, there was something else. *Music.* A cluster of melodic notes floated through the air—he reached for his sword.

Perin was ready to protect his sister, but Rhona didn't seem the least bit frightened. In fact, she was *smiling,* and her skipping accelerated, before turning into a jog.

"Quil!" she shouted.

Quickly, Perin ducked behind a large tree with ropey vines and spied around it to find a boy with short black hair and brown skin, close to their age. A flute similar to the one Perin had found earlier in Rhona's hand was in between the boy's— *Quil's*—lips. As Quil lowered the flute, he grinned back at Rhona.

Perin frowned. *This is what she's doing? Meeting a boy from another village?* He would have to put a stop to this, but the smile on her face—and seeing her free like this—filled him with doubt. Quil must have been the person who had made the crown for Rhona—the one Perin had fixed. Maybe this would just be for a little while—maybe when he returned from the Stone of Desire, Rhona wouldn't be coming out here anymore. Even if she did, he would protect her secret from Belen.

Quietly, Perin slipped away as swiftly as possible, then dashed back to the edge of his village so he could begin his journey. He hoped with all his heart that the Stone would answer him, but not for him—for his sister.

Three

Tavarra
Present Day

This place, this world, wasn't Tavarra's home—it never had been. Laith was but a place that took, and took, and took *everything*. Tavarra's heart was a bitter thing—wounded—feeling too many memories of the past or the future that could have been. Yet, there was guilt, too, because deep, deep inside was the tiniest fraction of relief, because the beast—*her* monster—hadn't come back. The murderess she hated and had never truly met, who could rip apart anyone and anything, was gone from her skin, her muscles, her nerves, her bones. It was a goodbye long overdue, but a goodbye nonetheless.

Gripping her necklace almost too tightly, she ran her fingers across the objects that were gifts from two miraculous friends—both gone now. A shell from a fierce and loving bat who had resembled a dark fairy, and a ring from a man who had put others before himself. Eza. Perin. One friend she had known for years, while the other … there just hadn't been enough time.

"One moment you're here and the next you're *gone*," Tavarra said softly, behind closed eyelids. Except she wasn't gone, she was still here. Alone.

Weeks ago, she'd trekked with Perin's sister, Rhona, to the Stone of Desire, which had saved her from herself. But even with the beast gone, she didn't feel whole. She felt *tired*.

She kept her eyes closed, waiting for the sounds about to rise at dawn. Behind her lids, she could see orange brightening the black. In the distance, hisses, tiny roars, and the flap of wings radiated. She gathered that beautiful memory of when she had been here last, with Eza.

Finally, Tavarra opened her eyes, meeting brilliant yellows, blues, oranges, and greens weaving with each other. Tiny dragons connected with her gaze. The lovely creatures swayed and glided effortlessly through the air, finding their own dance and rhythm, a ritual only they knew. One she wished she could figure out, but she wasn't a dragon. She was Tavarra, and she wasn't sure who or what she was anymore, besides a human who didn't know how to be one.

She was good at that. Not knowing how to just be. The beast she could never grow to love, and the dweller she had never truly accepted.

With a light touch, Tavarra brushed the seashell from Eza, the sapphire ring from Perin, the imaginary gift that she wished she had from her sister Nezarra.

"Breathe in, breathe out," Tavarra demanded of herself. "Gather their strength."

"You have strength, too, Tavarra," she whispered in a voice that would have been Eza's if she were there.

In answer, she let go of the necklace—it bounced against her chest before coming to a stop.

Averting her gaze from the dragons, Tavarra focused on the land around her. It was colorful with the hues of happiness. Bright pink sky, burning yellow suns, jubilant dragons, the grass a soft blue, flowered mountains in the distance.

Still, a heavy weight settled in her chest, drawing away any potential smile.

Tavarra ran a hand down her cheek and thought about what her next step would be. She didn't even know. Rhona had asked her to come back to Quil's village, practically begged. Perin's sister would have been there for a while now with Quil and Lana. Tavarra could go there. But she barely knew those people. A part of her still hated Rhona for knocking her out, which Tavarra felt had led to Perin's death. Yet, a stronger part of her couldn't help but be grateful for Rhona pushing her to seek out the Stone afterward.

Perin.

She was frustrated with him, too. Frustrated with him for asking Rhona to use her ability to make Tavarra pass out for a little while. But she couldn't bring herself to hate him, no matter how much she wanted to. Hating him like she had Brice would have made her feel stronger, yet she couldn't push her heart to beat in that direction. It would have made things much easier if she could. And without Eza—or anyone—to talk to, she felt … lost.

A flutter drifted across her palm, catching her off guard. Tavarra glanced down to find a yellow dragon spinning in circles near her fingertips, its long furry tail beating side to side. She flipped up her hand, and the dragon came to a stop and rested near the center of her middle finger. Its clawed feet lightly tapped against her skin.

Slowly, Tavarra raised the dragon upward, so its tiny black eyes met hers. "Would you have let Eza ride on you this time?" She wasn't sure if this was the same dragon that the bat had once attempted to ride, but she knew that Eza would have tried to hop on this one regardless.

She brought the furry dragon even closer to her face—it almost looked as though it was smiling at her, resembling a little ball of sunshine. "Be free and happy." She lifted her hand as high as it would go for the dragon to fly away.

The words had really been for herself more than anything, and she felt selfish about that.

Hoisting her pack over her shoulder, Tavarra left the fluttering dragons to their perfect family and walked away.

Tavarra had told Rhona before they went their separate ways that she was going to visit the sea for a while, but she still hadn't traveled anywhere near that direction. Perhaps she would, perhaps she wouldn't. She wanted to, but the last time she was there, Eza had been with her. In fact, all of Laith reminded her of the bat because they had trekked endlessly across the land together, just trying to survive or find the Stone of Desire. Her stomach growled—she couldn't remember the last time she had eaten. The incredible strength she'd once had from the curse was gone, so she felt off when she tried to hunt. Her claws were no longer there for her to just dig into her prey and easily tear it apart—she didn't have the sharp teeth to rip into the flesh, either. She now only had two human hands and two pathetic daggers.

What she needed was a bow. Or a sword—Rhona and Perin knew how to fight with theirs. But she had never really learned how to use that particular weapon.

Farther ahead, a bush covered in violet berries shook. Tavarra dropped down into a crouch and watched as a drogwai slowly walked out from inside it, sniffing at several leaves. The creature's triangular ears perked straight up on its oval-shaped head. Tavarra's mouth salivated for just a single taste of the delicate meat hidden beneath the fur. The drogwais weren't very fast creatures, so she lunged forward, barreling straight for it.

Tavarra's hand wrapped around the barely-there neck—she yanked the dagger out from her waistband and stared at the two beady eyes watching her. Her hand gripping the weapon tightly froze in midair, shaking. What was wrong with her?

She'd had no problem killing little creatures for food before.

A nauseous feeling consumed her, and she set the drogwai down as she tried to catch her breath. Instead of running away and trying to save its life, the stupid thing stayed beside her. And she let it, not saying a single word as she slipped the dagger back by her waist. Too tired to withdraw her shackles, she reclined against a gnarled fruitless tree as the night fell, dreaming that it was filled with pears or apples as she let herself fall asleep.

In the morning, Tavarra awoke to howls in the distance and rubbed at her scarred wrists. She turned over to reach for the drogwai, but the creature was already gone. It had given her a little bit of comfort that she had desperately needed. Her stomach shifted and growled, reminding her that she needed to eat.

She wished the drogwai would return because she was back to herself for the moment, and she could have eaten it now. *What a terrible thought...* And maybe she couldn't eat that specific one, but she did know what she could hunt down and consume instead.

As if hearing her thoughts, the howl grew closer. Tavarra would answer its call. She stood and wiped the dirt from her pants and rumpled the bush, so the branches crackled, and the leaves swished like a thunderstorm. "Over here!" she shouted.

A momentary silence took place before stomping sounded from behind her. Tavarra spun around as she withdrew both daggers, coming face to face with the creature she wanted—four horns, gray skin, golden eyes. *Jovkin.*

Despite the close proximity, she held no fear as she flung a dagger with accurate precision, piercing just below its throat. A gasp escaped the creature's mouth, and its eyes widened as blood spilled down its chest.

The jovkin yanked the blade out and tossed it to the ground as if it was nothing. Tavarra had one weapon left. She may not have her strength, but what she did have was her rage from what had happened to Eza. As the jovkin jolted forward, Tavarra whirled to the side, baring her teeth as though she were a beast. With a battle cry, Tavarra ran forward and brought her fist down as hard as she could, stabbing it directly in the chest, where the blade connected right with the heart. Body shaking with hatred, she took a step back and let the jovkin slump to its knees, before falling to the side.

Tavarra hovered over and stared down at the dead creature. It felt good—she felt vindicated. And what she decided to do then was eat and fill her stomach with as much as she could. The thing deserved it. As she cut and tore off pieces of the jovkin, for a moment, she thought that maybe she did have something more than human strength, but it was only the lingering anger that assisted.

Wiping her forearm across her forehead, she then started a small fire to roast the meat. This had been her fourth jovkin kill since Eza had died. And each one had her feeling better, until that emotion went away and turned back into a spiral of memories.

The smoke filtered inside her nostrils, and the meat began to blacken. She continued to eat and cook more and more until her stomach felt as though it would burst. She was full, but there was a taste for blood that still lingered on her tongue— for a vengeance that might not ever be satiated.

I wouldn't want that. Live your life, Tavarra. If Eza had been alive, that was what the bat would have spoken.

Tavarra flicked away the annoying thought of her dead friend's words, because that's what she was. Dead. Lifting her pack over her shoulder, she headed to a place where there would have to be another jovkin.

As she crossed over fallen branches, she trampled through small dips in the ground and leaped over a narrow stream. The uneven earth, mixed with rocky areas, had her stumbling a few times.

Finally, up ahead, she could see the peach trees—rows and

rows of them. Most were empty of fruit.

Just as she had earlier, Tavarra didn't even attempt to remain quiet. She already had her daggers in both hands, hoping to spot something.

"Come on," she whispered as she scanned the area, then yelled and slapped a tree. "Come on!"

In answer, the ground thumped from her left, and Tavarra turned to the side. A jovkin with two broken horns on his forehead whirled around, his gaze meeting hers. She hurled a dagger, not waiting for the creature to speak, charge, or hurt anyone else. The weapon struck true to the heart. It wasn't enough, not for her. She delivered the other blow, striking between the jovkin's eyes, just above the flattened nose. Dust rose as the body fell to the ground.

"Who's next?" Tavarra raged while moving to retrieve her daggers from the dead body. As she leaned down, two strong hands pushed her to the ground, pinning her.

"One less jovkin means more peaches for me, but you're not looking to kill only him, are you?" the male jovkin growled above her.

Tavarra didn't care, and most likely had a death wish, as she spat in his face, then slammed her leg between his. The jovkin howled and shifted back, leaving her enough time to crawl out and run.

Through the peach trees, she ran weaponless, before entering a more wooded area filled with some of the tallest trees she had ever seen, blooming large yellow leaves. As her breathing came out ragged, she assumed the jovkin would have given up, but she was wrong. After all, she had wanted to kill him.

Behind her, heavy grunts and growling drew closer, his steps increasing. She knew she couldn't beat the wicked thing. *Perhaps I should stop running. Perhaps I should just give in to being ripped apart.* The thundering footsteps sounded closer—something swooshed directly by her head. An arrow.

Tavarra's body almost froze, but she chose to keep running. Her head twisted in all directions as her feet stomped against the dirt, the pack on her back grew heavier, weighted. She couldn't find where the arrow had come from, then another one whizzed by.

Snap.

She hadn't realized what had happened until an agonizing scream sounded—coming from her. The fierce pain shot through her leg, and she dizzily looked down to find something clamped around her foot, crushing it, bringing about such intense hurt that she thought her appendage had come off. Tavarra stumbled to the ground, her head striking a rock. Her vision blurred when the pain at her temple and foot increased. The color black became all she could see, stealing away her sight. She waited for the jovkin—or an arrow—to take her down, whichever came first. As she floated away, Tavarra thought about the *Little Red Riding Hood* story Perin had told her. She wasn't a beast anymore, but maybe she wanted to be.

Four

Perin
Present Day

Perin was shrouded in a cloak of soil. His body was underground. He couldn't move, couldn't shout, all he tasted was dirt and despair and desperation. Why was he buried in the earth? *Why?*

Fuck. He clenched his eyelids tightly, bringing his anxious thoughts to the surface, *remembering*. Rhona came out from the depths—his sister—curly blonde hair, eyes the color of his, stubborn, his spark of sunshine. That's all he could envision as he tried, with frustration, to clear the blur and the pounding of his head. He needed to get to her and protect her from his bastard of a father. His father—Belen—*dead*.

His father was dead. The king of all things that had driven Perin mad, all the emotional pain his father had caused could now be *gone*. More memories drifted upward.

Rhona had done it—she'd killed Belen by using the prisms and her ability. Perin hadn't needed to protect her—she'd done it all on her own. At that moment if he could have smiled, he would have, but he couldn't.

Perin wiggled his shoulders to try and break free from the

dirt prison. Then he stopped and remembered something sharp sliding into his stomach—Thea had had a weapon. It had caused pain so fierce that it had cut off his breathing, suffocating him. The final light inside his body had been snuffed out, taking him to his death. The last thing he recalled before the light blinked out was a faint glow of orange. Not the shining rays from the two suns, but hair so tangerine that it had held the light for him until the darkness swept everything away. Tavarra. Someone he'd only grasped for moments, but his heart had already started to beat for her. A pounding he'd had for no other.

Something clamped inside his stomach, tightened so much that he felt like he would die all over again. He clenched his jaw, trying to stuff the pain right back down to wherever it had come from. But he was starving at the same time, just so fucking hungry. How long had he been down here, underground? Days? Weeks? Years? He was drowning in an ocean of dirt, and he had to get out.

Focus. Just focus.

Despite wanting to burst through the ground in a single swooping movement, Perin knew that wouldn't happen. So he jerked his arms, causing the ground to shift. It didn't budge as much as he wanted. He'd had it, fed up with the predicament he was now in. As he pushed and struggled, he also roared and shouted while specks of dirt clung to his tongue. The saliva tasted of a bittersweetness that he wanted gone.

Gritting his teeth, Perin hoped to all of Laith that he was digging the right way out. For all he knew, he could be traveling farther into the hellish dirt pit.

The soil grains packed his nostrils, his ears, and his mouth. What wasn't packed with this shit? It was as if he was made of dirt. Jaw clenching tighter, he punched and shuffled and wiggled until the soil became softer, looser, freer. His heart pumped with venom and endurance when his right hand broke through something. With desperation consuming him, he wiggled his fingers—the cool bite of air nipped at them and his palm.

Right there. Perin was right there. Even though he was so close, his body was tired, dizzy, and wanted to slump over for a little longer. *No.* He pushed his other hand upward, penetrating through the thick barrier. Gathering his remaining strength, he hauled himself up, head striking air. A low growl escaped his mouth as he moved his forearms against the ground to drag the rest of his body out before collapsing to the grass.

Perin was worn, spent, and could hardly breathe, but he sucked in the air as though it was water rehydrating him. The inhale must have been too hard because a string of coughs racked his body and he spat out chunks of dirt.

When he rolled over onto his back, he finally opened his eyes, letting the two suns' light pour onto him. Light that he'd never hoped so much for in his life to see, until right at that moment. Automatically, he reached for the sword at his side, only to find it wasn't there.

Breathe in. Breathe out.

Heavy thunder crackled from above, and he focused on the darkening sky.

What the fuck is going on? Pulling himself to his knees, Perin sat back on the heels of his boots. Specks of mahogany covered every inch of him. He stared down at the dirt he'd spat out, noticing something green entwined with it. Reaching for it, he found a clover hidden inside. Someone, most likely Rhona, had buried him with clovers? He tossed it down.

His eyes adjusted to his surroundings and widened at the familiar sight as mist fell from the sky. A meadow—his meadow. Clusters and clusters of clovers covered the field, all in full bloom, like always. Nothing new. He ran the tip of his tongue over his teeth and the roof of his mouth—something tasted different, but it wasn't the dirt.

Perin couldn't focus on that right now. "Rhona!" he

shouted. "Tavarra!" Running a hand through his hair, he thought of Eza, but wouldn't be able to call for her. Because she was dead. Because he hadn't been quick enough.

No one returned his shouts, no one at all. He needed to go back to his home and find them.

As he headed toward the village, his body was stiff with aches like it never had been before. Maybe his sister and Tavarra were there. They had to be. But how had he gotten to the meadow? Rhona couldn't have carried him, but Tavarra would have been able to. She'd done it before.

The rain stayed light as it came down, even though the thunder had ceased. Perin rotated his shoulders, cracked his knuckles, and popped his neck repeatedly while he wandered back home, passing the clusters of willow trees.

Inside the village, everything sat quiet—too quiet. Not a single chop of wood, not the sound of water swishing from clothes being washed—nothing. The cone-shaped tents all looked abandoned from the outside, and he wasn't sure what rested inside. Was everyone still under Belen's spell? *They should've woken up once Rhona defeated him, right?*

Perin lifted the curtain of the first tent, covered in tiny painted blue and red handprints. His gaze circled across the room with clothing sprawled about. It took him a moment to focus on the two bodies resting beside a rocking chair—a dark-haired woman and a child of four years old. Shriveled and dead—no breaths. Celia and Eric. Those were their names.

Dropping the opening of the tent, he moved to the next one and the next. All dead. No one had awakened or had their lives given back to them. With his heart pounding rapidly, he noticed the rain had stopped. Why was he even concerned about mist when his entire village was gone?

Belen had done this—his father was the one responsible. Perin should have done something sooner, but he hadn't known his father was going to suck the life out of everyone. He hadn't known it was happening until it was too late. Even then, he assumed it could all be reversed with the prisms.

The field.

He tried to run, but it turned into more of a hobble. His body was still trying to recover from the lack of movement he'd had below ground. As he edged toward the wide-open field, more willow trees outlined the grassy area. What if his father wasn't really dead, just as Perin wasn't? He pushed the dreaded thought back down.

To his relief, as his gaze swept anxiously across the grass, it landed on where Belen lay—rotting. His body rested on its side, head angled toward the sky, and his ponytail was mussed. Perin wished he could reach for his sword and decapitate him. If he had his weapon on him, he would not have only removed Belen's head, but stabbed him straight through the heart for good measure. Even Belen's and Thea's swords weren't in the field any longer.

Farther away, with her head at an odd angle, lay Thea. Bugs and worms ate away at her flesh. The areas of her skin that were still visible were a pale white shade, her lips tinted blue. Despite her shudder-worthy appearance, Perin felt no remorse at her death.

Thea should have known better, should have paid attention to her daughter more. Even when Perin tried to discuss anything with her, she would shush him. Shaking his head, he turned away and dropped to the balls of his feet. He ran his hands through his short hair with his eyes closed, thinking. If not here, then where would Rhona and Tavarra have gone to next? He'd told Rhona what to do if something happened to him. The Stone of Desire was exactly where they would have gone. But how long had he supposedly been dead? How much time had passed?

Perin's pack was still there. He opened it up and didn't find anything of importance. Rhona must have taken what she could, then left.

Throwing his pack down, he needed to get some things

together to go and find them. As quickly as he could, Perin ran in the opposite direction toward his cabin, ignoring any aches his body gave.

The cabin slid into view with its thick logs and uneven roof. The place never felt like his, even though he'd lived there with his father—and that was probably why.

Throwing open the door, he hurried inside his room and scrambled to find his other pack. His room still felt like someone else's. There wasn't much inside since they'd moved in two years ago. His old room had been different—there had been gadgets that he'd tried to build in a vain effort to stop his father. But in the end, he'd given up, knowing nothing would work.

Not dallying, Perin stuffed his pack with clothing and attached one of his spare swords at his hip.

Inside the dining area, he found spare jerky and added it to his bounty. He needed to hurry and get to the Stone of Desire. The directions were still embedded into his memory, even more so since the first and last time he'd gone to the Stone when it had failed to answer him.

As he wandered across Laith to the Stone of Desire, Perin wasn't afraid. He had one wish left, one hope, and that was to awaken the Stone. Dried mud coated his body, and he hadn't stopped to eat that day, no matter how much his belly demanded to be fed. He was too anxious with the specific goal in mind.

After treading through a lifeless swamp, he reached an area where leaves of orange and pink peeked through an opening of a bush. With the tip of his new blade, he moved the limb and stared ahead.

He followed the new colors and watched as black leaves slipped into his view, his heart pounding with something new and ferocious. Beads of sweat sprinkled across his forehead, and he swiped them away as he kept on moving.

Beneath the beams of the burning suns, he stopped in his

tracks, swearing he could see something. Chewing on his lower lip, Perin inched forward and sucked in a sharp breath. Before him, alabaster in color with an intricate rose-shaped design on top, rested the Stone.

Perin's face didn't brighten with a smile—instead, his frown deepened with determination. Breathing in and out, he walked at a brisk pace, trying to conceal his desperation.

When he stood in front of the Stone, he let out a heavy sigh and placed his hand on the rose-shaped top, rubbing his thumb against the grainy texture.

"I desire one thing and one thing only," Perin said, "and that's for you to rid this world of my father, for my sister, Rhona."

Gathering patience, he waited. And waited. And waited. The Stone didn't answer. Sometimes things had to be begged for, so Perin dropped to his knees and hugged the Stone, his hands not even able to wrap halfway around. Tears came then, the ones he'd promised would never come again. "Please. Please help her." He cried and cried, sitting there longer than he should have, curling on his side beside the Stone as the day bled to night and the night opened to day, asking it over and over again for help.

No answer came.

This time he didn't lie to himself when he said he would never cry again after that. He never did.

If there was any child left in him at all, the journey home took what was left inside of him. He knew then that wishes and hopes weren't answered and that cruelty would always win.

"Did the Stone answer you?" Belen asked right as Perin opened the front flap of the tent.

"The Stone doesn't answer humans anymore," Perin replied. "You already knew this."

"Turn around and remove your shirt then," Belen said with nonchalance. "All you did was waste time. I told you exactly how long to be gone, and yet you came back two days

Perin tightened his jaw and faced the other direction, awaiting his punishment.

Shrugging away the memory, Perin took a large bite of jerky. As soon as he bit into it and chewed, something akin to dirt rose to the surface. He spat it out and rubbed at his tongue, wondering if there had still been dirt in his mouth from before. There had been fruit in the house that was spoiled, but the jerky shouldn't have been. He'd have to find something else to munch on along the way and strive to ignore the pain in his stomach in the meantime.

But first, Perin touched the sword he now had by his side. Nothing stopped him from carrying out at least one wish: he would remove his father's head before leaving.

When he exited the village, Perin didn't look back once—there wasn't anything he could do, no one he could save. However, he made sure that even his father's dead body could never rise again.

At the lake, he came to a stop and filled his canteen with water, drank, and filled it again. Perin pulled out a set of clean clothes from his pack and tore the shirt from his head. His body froze when he looked down at his stomach. The wound was still there with a thick crusted-over scab, but it didn't look infected. He remembered his wounded leg—from the injury he'd let Rhona inflict—and pulled off his pants. The stitches were still there, but the gash was already healed, so he took the thread out after he stepped into the warm lake. While monitoring the area, he quickly washed off, trying to rid himself of dirt and inner demons, but only one rinsed away.

Perin reminisced about how he'd kept so many secrets over the years to make sure his sister remained safe, to protect her. Even with Tavarra, he tried to do what he thought was best for her at the time—because she would have been a distraction. He knew she couldn't have survived against his father with that prism in his hand. The choice he'd made was the right one because he would have rather died himself than have anything happen to Rhona or Tavarra.

Yet he hadn't died.

His stomach still ached, so he stretched up and lengthened his spine, but it only became worse. He needed to hunt down something to eat.

Climbing out from the lake, Perin slid the dry tunic over his still-wet body and tugged on a pair of pants. Then he washed the dirt from his boots as best he could and slid those on, too.

Howls sounded in the distance, capturing his attention, and he let his hand touch his sword. They slowly faded farther away, but the animalistic noises didn't sound like Tavarra's werewolf—it was something else.

The grip on his sword slackened, and he trudged ahead to where fruit trees sprinkled in a large circle. He plucked several pears and let his teeth sink into the thin skin. Almost as fast as he bit into it, he spat the chunk out and pulled the fruit away to wipe at his tongue. Taste of dirt again? He threw the pear down and bit into the other—that one tasted just the same. He spat that piece out as well, trying to get the flavor out of his mouth. Another and another he tried, followed by one more. They each tasted similar. Perin stopped and backed up to one of the trees, staring up at all the healthy fruits. Something was very, very wrong. And it wasn't the fruit—it had something to do with him.

Five

Tavarra

A loud crunch, followed by a slow creak, caused Tavarra's eyes to flicker open. She let out a groan when she moved her foot. It throbbed with intense pressure—so much pain that she wanted to expel everything in her stomach. Her eyes wouldn't adjust, and they fluttered shut just as two hands scooped her up from the ground. No one had carried her ever—not below the sea and not above. She hated it, but she didn't have enough strength to protest. Deliriousness filtered through her entire body, and she held back the scream that wanted to break out from her throat.

Tavarra could have sworn she had heard the flap of bat wings, could have sworn she heard the steady breathing of a certain man she had once tried to choke, then carried like a babe to save his life. But she knew it could be neither because they were both dead. She let whoever's—or whatever's— hands that were holding her carry and bring her to any life or death that awaited because, at that moment, she didn't care about anything except escaping the pain.

"Tavarra, you are strong," Eza said. "Not just because of what you can do, but because of your heart. You're a survivor, and not just because I'm here, but because of who you are.

Even if we hadn't found each other, you would have always found a way. Believe in that. Trust in that. Always."

Tavarra stared at Eza's gray eyes and two black braids. "I trust in you. That's all." She had learned who she could trust a long time ago, and it was only her friend.

"I do give off a certain impression, don't I?" Eza smiled and flew in circles around Tavarra's head.

Chuckling, Tavarra reached into the river and snagged a gold and violet fish. Her claws sliced open its belly. "That you do, Eza. That you do."

Tavarra pried her eyelids open and blinked several times as she tried to adjust to the light of the suns spilling in through a window. The beat of her heart seemed to reawaken as its thumps increased. She shifted to bring herself up to a sitting position but slumped back down. Her head fell to the right, where her gaze latched onto a face she didn't recognize.

She stilled and let out a small gasp, jerking forward. Her hurt foot twisted in the wrong direction, and she bit her tongue to transfer whatever pain she could to that area.

"Whoa!" the man said and gently pushed her down by the shoulders. His face looked a little older than hers, with dark eyes and thick lashes. Chestnut-colored hair fell past his shoulders against olive skin. Her heart kicked up another notch, and she jolted forward again.

"Stop doing that," he said softly, holding onto her upper arms and not letting go. "You're going to make your leg worse if you keep at it."

"If you don't release my arms, I will find a way to rip your next breath from you," Tavarra seethed. She didn't know this man, and she didn't want to be in his shelter—or his bed.

He released his grasp and took a seat back in a chair. "You got caught in my trap. And how surprised I was to find a woman there. I've been trying to catch a certain jovkin and a beast for a while now."

Tavarra remembered the jovkin chasing after her. "The

one after me?"

"He's dead, but that wasn't the jovkin I've been waiting for." He tapped the ends of his fingers together and surveyed her face.

She wanted to ask why he was after a certain jovkin, but she didn't want to tell this stranger any part of her past interactions with the creatures, either. Instead, she just said, "Oh." Another groan escaped her lips as her leg throbbed like it had been set on fire. A thought made her uneasy—was her leg even still there? "Is my leg...?" She shifted a little to see if she could see her appendage.

The man propped a booted foot on his opposite knee, and his relaxed position angered her. "Your leg's still there, and you're fine. Nothing's broken. You might not want to move quickly like that again if you want it to heal properly."

Despite the pain, a sense of relief washed over her that her foot was still there.

"You're lucky it didn't shatter anything, though," he continued. "It'll take a few days to mend, and I've got some healing ointment that will speed up the process."

On instinct, Tavarra wanted to narrow her eyes. Why was this man attempting to help her when she didn't know him at all? But it was his fault for having traps set in the forest. Most men were fools. And when she thought of fools, she couldn't help but think about Perin once more. The only good man she knew was Quil, and maybe that was because they had both been betrayed in a sense. There was a kinship she felt for him, even though she had barely spoken any words to him. Tavarra wondered if he had forgiven Rhona for leaving him behind. She knew he had. Just as she would have forgiven Perin. Perhaps.

Tavarra stayed silent and gazed down at her clasped hands. A quilt—stitched with a tree straight down the center and suns surrounding it—covered her and the bed.

"My sister made that quilt, but she isn't alive anymore,"

the man said when she didn't open her mouth to speak. He had lost a sister? Like she had… "Anyway, that was a while ago. I'm Ian, by the way. And your name?"

For now, she would play nice, especially when she knew she wouldn't be able to bring herself to walk until he helped take care of her leg. "Tavarra." If Eza were there, she would have been kind, would have been grateful, would have said for Tavarra to thank him in other ways.

Tavarra's throat felt dry as she took a deep swallow and adjusted her upper body. "Do you have any water?"

He tilted his head in the direction beside her. "Right there on the table."

She wanted to roll her eyes as she picked up the glass and guzzled the water down. It wasn't enough, though. Her thirst still lingered, but she didn't request a second helping.

The silence was awkward. She'd had comfortable quiet with others, but nothing like this. *Is he going to stay in here the whole time?*

"You don't come from around here, do you?" Ian asked, his tone seeming to already know the answer.

Her gaze did narrow then, because she could read someone well enough when they were trying to play some sort of game. And she wasn't one for that. She cocked her head. "Why do you say that?"

Ian lifted a lock of his own brown hair. "The orange is very noticeable."

"Oh." Tavarra's shoulders relaxed as she ran a hand through her ratty tangles. Her hair had fallen out from the leather strap and needed to be washed. In fact, her whole body practically demanded it—the smell of dirt and grime on her skin assaulted her nose.

As she stared at Ian with his pretty face—all angles and bushy eyebrows—and his lean body, she thought she might have judged him too soon. It was a habit that was hard to break, but maybe she could try … for Eza.

"Are you alone here?" Tavarra asked, taking stock of her surroundings. In front of her, against the wall, rested a table with different weapons sprawled out across the top, and beside it stood a dresser with drawers. On the wall, to her left, hung a wooden board with different daggers attached, as if they'd been thrown at it. Paintings lined the wall to her right, all in crooked directions.

"Yes, just me. My partner was killed a year ago, and he didn't deserve it." His jaw locked, cheeks reddened with anger trying to stay hidden. Tavarra couldn't meet his gaze. Death was something no one could get used to, least of all her.

"I'm sorry," she finally said, even though those two words really didn't mean anything at all. It was just something one said for comfort, yet it wouldn't take away the emotions.

"That's what the traps are for."

"The jovkins seem to do what they want." That's all she said. She didn't want to go into detail about Eza, only wanted to get her foot healed so she could venture elsewhere.

"May I?" Ian asked, pointing at her foot.

"All right." Tavarra knew she sounded suspicious, but he was only touching her foot. She needed to stop.

He moved toward the blanket with a friendly smile and drew the quilt up. A white cloth bounded her leg, and he carefully unwrapped it, causing only a minimal stinging sensation. "The ointment is already starting to help—it's looking much better. No sign of infection."

As he added some more ointment to her ankle, she thought about weeks ago when she was taking care of an incredibly stubborn man who *did* have an infection. Was she being as stubborn as him right now? Tavarra reached for her throat to grasp the necklace and stopped. She ran a hand across her skin as if the objects were still there. But they weren't—her necklace was gone.

Ian stuck a hand inside his pocket and pulled out her necklace, dangling it in front of her. "Is this what you're looking for?"

Lowering her eyebrows, Tavarra reached her hand out to yank it back. She didn't like anyone touching her things, and that necklace was only meant for her.

He pulled it away before she made contact and pushed it back into his pocket. "No, I don't think so."

"Give it to me," she growled, shooting forward. Even though she was now human, she could have jabbed him in the throat, but the throbbing in her leg tore an anguished shout from her. Before she had time to move again, Ian was on her, pinning her down.

"I knew it was you." He held her arm down as he grabbed for a rope that was already bound to the bed and tied up her other one. Bucking and wiggling didn't help her, not when he was stronger, because she was too tired and weak. Then he took the other wrist and repeated his previous movements. She wanted her daggers that had been left behind—she wanted her claws.

After Ian finished, he straddled her on the bed, pressing his face too close to hers. She could smell the scent of something he'd smoked earlier. "Do it!" he demanded.

Tavarra didn't know what sort of sick game he was trying to play, but she would figure out a way to rip off his manhood and shove it down his throat. "Do what?"

"Change into the monster," he demanded, removing himself from the bed and crossing his arms.

Her whole body froze, only her heart continued to pump as she stared at the crazed eyes of this bastard. A man who somehow knew a secret she once carried around with her.

"Change into the monster!" he shouted this time. "So I can kill the beast who murdered my partner."

Six

Perin

A cramp twitched in Perin's stomach, and he lifted his shirt to inspect the scab from the stab wound. It didn't appear any different. But why would it? He'd just looked at it not long ago at the lake. The thought reminded him of the scars on his chest, and it would just be another mark to add to the collection. At times he'd wished his wounds would have closed up the way Rhona's had started to, so there wouldn't have been as many reminders. Even so, a single scar from his father would have been one too many.

Each mark his father bestowed on him he remembered clearly. No matter how much he wanted them to, the memories wouldn't fade in the slightest. Absently, he rubbed at the scar right under his collarbone—it was the one he most wished would fade.

"This one is for you still asking about your mother."
Then there were more and more that followed.
"This one is for you speaking up for Rhona."
"This one is for you wasting time with gadgets."
"This one is because you lied for Rhona."
"This one is because you defended Rhona."
"This one is because you backtalked me."

The list went on and on, and sometimes Belen would slice over the ones that had already scarred as though to show Perin that nothing could ever truly heal. Perin chose to keep his distance from everyone. He didn't like to be touched and didn't like anyone to be too near unless it had been on the field with a sword in his hand.

The only one, aside from Rhona, who'd gotten closer was Tavarra. And in a sense, she knew more truths about him than Rhona did—he'd told her about his scars. Yet it had taken all his inner strength to not tell her that a touch from anyone could trigger momentary flashbacks of his father.

Something inside his stomach beat like a heavy drum, harder than before. He removed his hand from his chest and lifted his canteen to his lips, drinking down the fluid. The pain stopped, and he hoped it would be more than briefly. Could it be possible that his stomach was mending from the outside, but not on the inside? That wouldn't make any sense, though—he just needed to eat.

Despite the taste of dirt, he plucked another pear and forced himself to eat it as he started the journey to the Stone of Desire. As he walked, the thumping in his stomach stayed away while he chewed on a piece of jerky. He could ignore the taste if he had to.

The moons in the sky were already starting to shift upward as the suns floated down. He'd hoped he would have had enough time to make it before night arrived, but he'd just have to wait until the following day. Something scurried beside a dying tree that looked to have recently fallen. It was Perin's lucky day. He leaped onto the broken trunk and swung his sword down, the rabbit's body splitting almost into two.

Quickly, he put together a small fire. Not the best, but it would do. He plucked the rabbit up by its ears to begin skinning the fur away from the flesh. But he stopped, catching a whiff of blood and flesh. His eyelids closed as he salivated over how wonderful it smelled. He thought about Tavarra, remembering how she'd eaten the rabbit without cooking it in the forest. Maybe just a taste to see how it would be—he'd never tried it before. It was messy as he buried his hand into the soft flesh, but he didn't care as he brought the insides to his mouth and groaned when the raw meat touched his tongue. It was delicious, filling his taste buds with its potent flavor, and he didn't know why he hadn't tried it before. With a smile, he lifted the carcass to his lips and devoured the rest.

Perin had woken at the same time as the suns. He moved and didn't stop, except to wash his face at a narrow stream and fill his canteen. His stomach still felt full from the night before, but he shoved a pear into his mouth to keep his strength. He hadn't thought about it until then, but there hadn't been a strange taste when he'd eaten the meat, not like now as he bit into the fruit.

After making it through the uneven territory and up and down stony hills with rough edges, Perin came to a familiar muddy swamp—one he'd crossed before. He sighed in relief because he wasn't that far away—unless the Stone had somehow vanished since he'd last seen it. As he entered the cool brush of the sloshy mud, the sludge only came as far as his waist, but it was still a thick consistency, making it difficult to cross. A sense of dread washed over him—he was too late, and Rhona and Tavarra wouldn't even be there.

Letting out a loud grunt as his feet planted to the bottom with each step, he pushed himself hard to make it that last inch and pull himself out.

Up, down, over, duck under—keep moving. Thorny bushes scraped at his arm and sliced holes into his tunic as he used his sword to get through the brambles. The suns stayed high, throwing down their heated rays, bringing perspiration to Perin's skin. He wiped the back of his neck and forehead as he passed leaves of orange, pink, and black, until finally, he came upon what he was looking for.

Years. It had been years since he'd been there last, but everything about it appeared the same. The Stone was still in the same position, but his sister and Tavarra weren't there. He'd already begun to suspect that, but his shoulders slumped anyway when he realized it was only him and the Stone. Once again. Déjà vu.

Rhona was okay now that his father was dead—he had to hold onto that. What he didn't have an answer to was Tavarra. She may or may not be a human, but she had to be alive. And if she were still the beast, then Rhona could knock her out with her ability if need be. There were too many questions for which he had no fucking answers.

He stood there too long, staring at the Stone, not really knowing what he was doing until he put himself first, for once, and asked himself the one question he never really had time to think about, "What is it you desire?"

"To be happy," he answered, knowing deep down that was something he'd always wanted. Everyone in the village had told him he frowned too much, but no one ever asked why.

A pain so deep and fierce yanked at his stomach, making him unable to catch his breath. He closed his eyes and stumbled toward the Stone of Desire and pressed his hand upon the rose-shaped top, knowing good and well that it wouldn't answer him. But he asked anyway, in a soft voice that he hadn't used since he was a child, "What is wrong with me?"

Like that, in answer, a vibration shook under Perin's boots. Little pebbles skidded in jagged lines side to side. Taking a hard swallow, Perin backed up, lips parted, as the Stone rose from the ground, going up to great heights. It took a lot to shock Perin, and this was one occurrence—besides Tavarra turning into the beast—where he couldn't get his thoughts straight. Two long arms shot out from the Stone, followed by two legs, the rose shape becoming its back. Something peaked through from what must have been shoulder blades—a bald, alabaster head.

On instinct, Perin unsheathed his sword but didn't budge from his spot. He'd seen a lot of things, a lot of creatures, but never something like this. Dangerous, beautiful, and strange— all at the same time.

Then two lids opened to crow-colored eyes, so deep and dark that Perin would never look at the color black the same way again. He expected a nose and a mouth to appear from somewhere, but neither did.

"What do you desire?" a demanding voice asked, catching him off guard.

Perin searched around through the trees, not seeing anyone else except this stone creature.

"What do you desire?" the voice boomed louder, and this time Perin knew it was coming from the Stone inside his own head as he clasped one side of his skull.

"I thought you didn't answer to humans anymore," Perin said bitterly. "Where were you when I needed you for my sister?" The anger inside him bubbled to the surface. The damned stone could have helped him with Rhona!

The Stone cocked its head as though only it knew a secret. "You do not know, do you?"

"Know what?" He dropped his hand from the side of his head but didn't lessen his grip on his sword.

"That you are no longer human."

"*What?*" Perin's eyes widened, and he bit his lower lip. What had happened to him underground?

"You woke in the meadow of clovers blessed by the Goddess," the Stone began. "It can give life a second chance if the land so chooses. Only this life is one that yearns for a taste of something darker."

"I didn't ask for that." Perin didn't relish in the idea of

being dead and rising up from the ground again. It reminded him of too many tales that he and Rhona would tell each other before bedtime when they were younger.

"Perhaps not, but your body did."

"Then, I desire to be rid of it."

"I cannot reverse it because, deep down, that is not what you really desire. But"—the Stone edged closer—"if you desire death, there is a sword right there, in your hand."

"Where can I find this so-called goddess you spoke of?"

"She exists no longer." The Stone crawled backward, before coming to a stop, its dark gaze meeting Perin's. "However, you do desire happiness, and there might be another option for a cure."

"What is it?"

"There is a lavender lake on the other side of the sea, in a place called Kova. Bottle a sample of the liquid, bring it to me, and I shall see what I can do."

"I know where the sea is, but I've never heard anyone talk of this place before." Perin's village never had reason to visit the ocean often, let alone venture across it.

"Most, or possibly all, have not returned to speak of it." The Stone spoke again before Perin could challenge the answer. "Cross the sea, then head south until you pass through bramble with silver thorns."

"Then what?"

"You will know."

With those final words, the Stone pulled its arms back, tucked its head as it folded in on itself, before shrinking back down into the earth.

"How the fuck am I supposed to cross a sea?" Perin called. No answer came, of course.

He'd originally come to the Stone of Desire to look for Rhona and Tavarra. Instead, he had an answer about himself that he didn't quite know how to unravel. Yet he was given a possible solution.

If Rhona wasn't here, then she would have gone back to Quil's village. He hoped Tavarra would have, too, but knowing her, she may have gone off on her own somewhere else.

For the time being, he would need to find his sister on his way to the sea.

Seven

Tavarra

"*Sister, you're so headstrong,*" *Nezarra said, dragging her emerald hair over her shoulder before it floated back upward. "You may think that being down here is a vicious thing, but out of the water, it can be so much worse.*"

Tavarra let her sister's words sink in. She always tried to be objective, but she just couldn't bring herself to agree with Nezarra. Besides, how would she know, anyhow? "This place doesn't feel like home to me, sister. I hate it. I've met someone on land, and he helps me dream about more."

Her sister rolled her eyes, placing a hand on Tavarra's bare shoulder. "Dreams are delusions, and even though you attempt to be distant, you still tend to trust too easily. There is only one who you need to trust, Tavarra, and that is yourself."

That was the thing that Nezarra didn't understand—she fully trusted herself and knew that Brice was a good man. "And you? I've always trusted you, dear sister."

"And that brings me honor. I trust you, too." Nezarra sighed, tiny bubbles escaping her mouth. "Just please don't lose focus on your life."

Tavarra thrashed forward in bed, slick with sweat. Before she could go any farther, she was hauled back by the rattling sound of the two binds that held her wrists, preventing her from escaping.

Ian—the fool she wanted to rip apart—had replaced the ropes with chains after they had started to split because of her constant jerking. She wasn't one to sit still and cry for her life—her blood boiled with anger.

Tavarra stared at the manacle latched to her left wrist, and it was such a recognizable sight. The chains should have brought her fear since they were stronger than cloth or rope and would be harder to escape. But it was the familiarity of the iron holding her as she slept that gave her comfort. There were nights when she still bound herself to a tree using the chains because it somehow helped her rest better.

It had been days. Days. Days. And more days that had passed. Tavarra felt grimy, smelly, tired, more so than when she originally came to this shelter. Her ankle no longer hurt since Ian continued to coat the area with the healing ointment. This man made no sense, and she wanted to tear his head off. Ian knew about the beast, but wouldn't explain more to Tavarra besides her monster killing his lover. Yet he still treated her leg daily. He was most likely afraid she would die from an infection before he could meet the beast. However, he would be waiting a long time for that.

A part of her did feel awful for what had happened, but she couldn't hold onto guilt if it wasn't her who had meant to do it. The beast was gone, and no matter how much she wanted to revive it to kill this crazy man, she couldn't rouse the monster. It was dead.

What she wanted, at that moment, was her necklace back. He had laid it on the table in front of her as if teasing her with it.

The door swung open, and Ian walked in, carrying a glass of water. Her mouth was so dry and full of thirst. He had only given her one meal a day along with water, and her body was becoming weak.

As she leaned forward for him to tip the glass of water into her mouth, he pulled it back. "Tut. Tut."

More than anything, she wanted to chop certain body parts off him before stabbing him in the throat. She was livid.

"Enough days have gone by," he continued, setting the glass on the side table. "I'll give you some water, but you're going to have to change first."

"I've told you over and over that I *can't*!" she seethed. "And each time, you fail to listen to me. I don't have the curse anymore!"

She knew Ian had this idea in his head that if he mended her leg, she would be able to change. But she couldn't turn an apple into a pear, just as she wouldn't be able to do this.

"You *will* figure out a way to make yourself turn, or you can lie here for the rest of your life." He struck the wall, causing one of the crooked paintings to crash to the floor. "You killed someone I loved. I want to deal head-on with the beast and not have to murder a human woman."

"Either way, it would still be me you're killing, even if I could turn into the beast!" She paused to think about what he had said. Tavarra had murdered his partner, and from what Eza had told her, she had ripped apart and eaten a lot of humans. When she woke up from being the monster the following day, Tavarra never remembered anything. Nothing. Not even if she woke up beside the dead bodies.

"Look," she said in a resigned manner, wishing she could at least remember the face of the man she had killed. "Whatever the monster did, I didn't choose to do that, and if I could undo it, believe me, I would. There are a lot of things I would undo. But if you want to kill me, then you're going to have to just do it, because I can't turn into the beast."

Ian shot toward her, leaving Tavarra no time to think. He held a blade so close to her eye that if she moved even the slightest bit, the knife would do real damage. She withheld the tremble aching to run up her spine as she stared at the weapon.

She wanted to rip it away and shove it into *his* eyeball.

"My partner went into the woods with another man to track you down for a reward." His smoky breath hit her nostrils. "I found his body, torn and mangled. The man who was with him had hurried away, then informed me that an orange-haired woman had changed into a beast. And what luck I had that you came straight into *my* trap."

"Then your partner shouldn't have been foolish enough to go after a monster in the middle of the night!" It was his lover's fault for trying to go out and kill her. She didn't care that her words to Ian were terrible, because this fucker had her chained to the bed for days and wouldn't hand her any water. The young sea dweller she used to be would have been ashamed of her words, but that girl was swimming somewhere far down in her heart—lost.

"You have only today to do it before I take you somewhere that will reverse the curse and make you become the beast." He lifted himself from the bed with a smirk on his face, still holding his dagger out.

She smiled a glorious smile then—even if she were to lose an eyeball, it would be worth it. "You can't. The one place you can go to doesn't answer to humans anymore. So it would seem we are both out of luck."

Ian brought the knife up once more and slammed it down. She hated herself for flinching, and she was prepared to shout in pain, but the blade had punched through the feathered mattress, directly beside her head.

He yanked it back out as though he had the victory. "We're going to search for the Stone of Desire right now. And if it doesn't pan out, then we'll find another way." From his pocket, he retrieved the key and unlocked the manacle around her right wrist.

Tavarra gathered up all the strength she could muster and waited for him to insert the key into the other lock. When he did, she yanked as hard as she could on her left wrist, while slamming her other fist into his face. It fazed him only for a moment before he lunged at her. She kicked him in the chest, the pain only minimal in her foot. Swiftly, she turned to unlock the chain, but she had somehow broken it from the bed, causing her eyes to widen.

Ian thrust a fist into her stomach, and she drove her knee into his face. She didn't hesitate as she found an opportunity and bolted straight out the door. The shelter appeared small as she ran out into a sitting room with a dilapidated front door. At least she hoped to the suns that it was the front door ahead. Tavarra lifted the bolt and threw it open just as Ian came storming out of the room.

With whatever energy she had stored inside her, she ran and shouted, mostly curses to get anyone's attention. She didn't know where she was exactly because there were no other cabins near Ian's. The area was secluded, where no one would hear her curses. But would they have helped anyway? They might have been just like Ian.

She needed a dagger, a bow, a sword, something besides her fists and a broken manacle dangling from her wrist. Silently, she cursed herself for not grabbing a weapon from the table in the room. For the moment, she used her weakened legs, attempting to pump them across the grass, her feet stinging as they hit sharp branches and pointy pebbles.

It had only been days since Tavarra had been outside, but she felt like it was all new to her as she sprinted across the ground. Heavy footsteps pounded behind her, and although she had wanted so badly to become human, for the first time, she truly regretted not having the curse. Her strength, her speed—*everything*—was missing!

The *thump, thump, thump* grew closer, the sounds heavier. She darted to the side, right as two hands caught her and shoved them both to the ground. Her body collided first, then her head struck next to a silver trap, like the nuisance that had wounded her leg—one of the causes for all this.

She couldn't let her mind fold around what it would feel like to get her head smashed by the trap—she already knew it would bring a swift, but cruel, death.

Ian pinned Tavarra down as she rolled to her back.

"Change!" he shouted. "Do it now! You took Les away from me!"

Tavarra's anger withered to something else, and she didn't know what to do. Maybe she should just let this man kill her, but she couldn't give him what he wanted. Even if she could, she wouldn't become the beast just for him to get his revenge. If she got the curse back, the beast would slash Ian to pieces, sending him to wherever his lover now was. Perhaps that was what he wanted.

"I can't," she whispered, gritting her teeth.

"Then, I'm sorry." He raised the knife, and she waited for it to slam down to take all her inner torment away.

When a heavy beating came through the forest, Ian glanced up just as something rushed forward and knocked him to the ground.

Tavarra's gaze focused and landed on something gray with four horns on its head, golden eyes, and distinctly male. *Jovkin*.

As he stalked toward her, she had no way to defend herself.

Eight

Perin

Perin left the Stone of Desire needing to find Rhona more than ever. He pressed his hands to his stomach, feeling the scab. His body was still trying to mend the wound. He'd died. He really had. And something … something *unnatural* had brought him back from the dead … something *wrong*. He wasn't a human anymore. What the fuck happened to him? What the fuck *was* he?

He needed to get to his sister and make sure she was okay before he headed out on this quest to fix himself—if that was even possible. No, he could do it. He had his sword, he had his wit, and he had a reckless side to him that never truly cared if he died.

All the nights he stayed up when the village was asleep to practice with his sword, and all the early mornings he'd woken to do the same, would be worth it. He'd have to welcome the challenge and know he could do it without failing.

It would take several days to get to the village, then a little longer to arrive at the sea, but he could do it.

The days to the village felt like hell, and the nights even longer. His stomach started to act up once again. He'd held off eating because he knew the taste of dirt would be there. There were a few apples he'd plucked and stuck into his pack but he hadn't yet touched them. His eyes fluttered, and he stopped near a tree, doubling over. He had to eat.

Opening his pack, Perin fished out a piece of jerky and one of the apples. The apple was the worst, with each bite tasting fouler, yet he forced it down. However, his stomach didn't feel the least bit satiated.

The jerky was a little better but still tasted of dirt. He stopped chewing when a sound clicked nearby—a twig snapping in half. Perin jerked up his head and withdrew his sword, knowing good and well what it must be as he scanned the peach trees. A feeling poured over him that he didn't want to think about—a small bat in which he'd tried to save but couldn't.

Perin skulked through the grass, lacing between trees. He could hear the heavy breaths of the jovkin. The creature would stay hidden until Perin drew closer. But he knew a way to make it come out.

"Mmm. I may just build my own village here, right where the peach trees grow." He plucked one from the branch and brought the fruit to his nose, taking a deep inhale. "Peaches should only belong to humans, after all."

One, two, three, he counted silently in his head. When he got to four, he smiled and whirled out of the way, raising his sword as a jovkin barreled past, missing him.

"You will be my dinner tonight as I dine on several peaches," the jovkin growled.

"That is quite the premonition, but I think you might be wrong about that."

The jovkin's nostrils flared against its flat nose. Long scars ran down the creature's temple, all the way to its chest. Someone had wanted to play with this jovkin before, too.

As the creature rushed forward, Perin grabbed a dagger from his hip and let it fly hard and fast, striking the jovkin straight between the eyes. Then he shoved his sword right through the heart. It may have not been the one who had eaten Eza, but the kill was for her anyway—for those other bats that this jovkin could have potentially murdered. If there were any left.

He yanked out his sword and watched the jovkin fall to the ground. Blood leaked out from the wounds, and he pulled the dagger from the head. His stomach twitched as the metallic scent filled his nostrils.

Perin pressed his tongue to the roof of his mouth as he stared at the dead jovkin. The hunger stirred, no longer restless as it built and built. He'd never eaten a jovkin before. Something about their body structure was too similar to humans. But right then and there, he didn't care.

Maybe he could try cooking pieces. Perin raised his sword and brought it down, slicing the head clean off, blood pooling out from the open wounds. The scent of meat became stronger, and he knew he couldn't bring himself to wait for it to cook. The raw meat from the rabbit earlier had been wonderful, and as he dipped his hand into the bloody flesh, there was a rush of disgust. But as he placed the fresh meat on his tongue, there was no comparison. This was worldly.

He chewed and swallowed—the feeling almost beautiful. It was what he'd craved, what his intestines had yearned for, what his very essence needed to survive.

The disgust disintegrated because his stomach no longer ached, and the body would have been left there to rot anyhow. Relishing the moment, he ate as much as he could, leaving entire areas with nothing but bone.

Blood lingered on his hands, and he thought about licking them clean, yet that very thought horrified him. But why was he repelled by that and not with what he'd just done? Regardless, he had to get the blood off. He rubbed his palms over and over on the trees, trying to erase the crimson, leaving stinging scuff marks behind.

All he wanted now was to hurry before his stomach started hurting again, so he walked until he found a place to rest for the night.

✦

"Perin, I need you to take Rhona to find the dark prism," Belen said. "I can't go there. It's taken longer than expected, but my prism feels her energy is complete."

"Yes, Father."

"When the two of you come back, you will put the blade to her heart and kill her."

"Yes, Father." Perin needed to agree to whatever Belen said because this was his time now. His and Rhona's chance.

"You haven't had to be punished in a while." Belen smiled. "I've grown most proud of you now that you've seen the ways."

"I want you to continue showing me the ways," Perin lied.

"Tomorrow will be the day."

Perin took a deep breath and sat up, holding his head, trying to escape the memory of his father. The suns had risen in the sky—it was already morning. Pushing the dream away, he headed to find Rhona.

As he neared Quil's village, he stopped by the river and quickly washed his face and body, wiping away any sign of blood or dirt. Once he got dressed, he headed toward the village, hoping to find Rhona or even Quil, but there was no sign of them. While at the river, he'd expected them to possibly be there, but they could be inside Quil's or Lana's home.

He drew closer, the cabins sliding into view, and sounds of people working echoed from inside the village. Just as he passed a few trees cloaked in thick moss, a woman stepped onto the path. Her dark hair was pulled into a single braid, and she wore a tunic and trousers—familiar.

She whirled around, catching his gaze with hers. Even though she couldn't hear, he knew she felt his presence, his vibrations.

Her eyes widened, her lips parted, and her brow lowered a fraction of an inch.

"You're not … you can't be…" Lana's words came out muffled, and the tone of her voice soothed him. It was something he didn't know he needed until that moment. "Can you?"

He'd been alone since he crawled out from the ground, except for interactions with things that he hadn't wanted to deal with.

Perin hadn't known Lana long, but she'd healed him when he needed help. In those few moments, she'd talked to him about life in the village as she'd stitched up his leg. She'd seen his scars, too, but never once asked what had happened to him.

"I think you still wouldn't have been able to get me on my back this time." He almost smiled as he shifted closer.

"Probably not, but Tavarra would have been." Her grin changed quickly to one of concern. "What's going on?"

"I'm alive, and I'll explain it all to you later, but is my sister here? I need to see her before I leave, just to make sure she's okay."

Lana lowered her brow completely and took several steps forward. "She's fine, but she and Quil aren't here. They left a little while ago to return the prisms, then they were going to journey for a bit before coming home. I don't think they'll be back for maybe another week."

He breathed a sigh of relief. Maybe this was for the better because now he knew she was safe, and she wouldn't be able to try and come with him. But a part of him wished she could—she was the voice of comfort. However, something was festering inside of him—something he would push to the back of his mind.

"And what did you mean by leaving?" Lana asked.

Perin quickly explained to her everything that had happened from waking up below ground, to going to the Stone of Desire. He left out his desire for fresh meat because that wouldn't do either of them any good.

There was one thing he'd waited to ask about—one person. He couldn't hold back any longer. "What about Tavarra? Is she here?"

Lana bit her lip and shook her head. "She never came back here."

"Oh..." He should have expected that. "Is—"

"If it helps," Lana interrupted, "the Stone did strip her of the curse. Rhona says she's human now."

The side of his lips tilted upward, and he dropped his shoulders. "That's all that matters. I'll possibly see you around."

"Whoa." She blocked his path, and a pleasant scent struck his nose. He pushed it away. "Where are you going?"

"I need to do what the Stone asks if I don't want to rot from the inside out, or whatever the fuck is going on." He thought about what would happen if he didn't make it and came up with a conclusion that would have to do. "You also can't tell Rhona I'm alive when she returns, not unless I make it back."

"No, there you are trying to protect her again. No more lies."

"It's not a lie. You're just withholding information."

"Perin." She narrowed her eyes. "You're just as stubborn as I remember."

"Apparently I can't help it. Even in death."

"You're not dead. And I'm going to come with you."

Yet, he wanted to say. Not dead *yet*.

"Wait right here," she continued. "I'll grab some things. Even though I hate it, I promise I'm not going to tell Emma or anyone else about you being alive."

Perin gave her a brief nod as she turned around to go back into the village. This was the perfect opportunity to leave, and he took it. Lana didn't need to get caught up in the shit that he was in, and if something happened to her, it would affect Rhona and Quil. He didn't care about the Quil part, but he couldn't hurt Rhona again.

His sister was safe, Tavarra was human—there was nothing else he wanted, except for him to go back to how he had been. Even if that meant never finding happiness.

Nine

Tavarra

Tavarra glanced down at Ian's body. He had been knocked out cold by the jovkin—the one who was walking toward her. Ian's knife had fallen to her left, and she hurried to scoop it up, then threw it as hard as she could at the jovkin. Her heart beat furiously as he jolted to the side, causing her to miss.

There had to be something else she could use. She backed up, searching the ground for anything, a broken branch, *something*. As her back struck the tree, she decided she would just have to use her fists and her legs. She swung a fist, then a leg.

The jovkin's flat nose crinkled upward, his determined expression becoming confused as he held up a hand. "Wait."

Wait? She wouldn't wait to listen to anything this foolish creature said. Narrowing her eyes, she held up her fists and moved closer. The jovkin didn't come toward her—instead, he picked up Ian's limp body and tossed him over his shoulder.

"Put him down *now*!" Tavarra seethed. If anything, she would tie Ian to the bed and let him see how it felt.

The jovkin's golden eyes widened in surprise. "He tried to kill you. There are traps spread out all over the forest. If you want to fight, you fight true, not set traps so it makes it unfair."

This was true, but Ian was probably a crazed man before he had even met her. "Are you not listening—"

With quick motions, the jovkin lifted Ian's head and snapped it, the bones making a loud crunching sound. Tavarra tightened her fists and inhaled sharply. The death didn't quite bother her, because he had it coming. If she'd had a weapon, she would have done it by her own hand, instead of running out of the shelter.

Tavarra took a step back as her mind cleared and she realized exactly who she was looking at—she hated the jovkin species. Hated every single one of them, hated this one, had killed them, but she couldn't move fast enough.

Then she remembered the table across from her bed with weapons sprawled across, ones she should have grabbed before running out of the shelter if she'd only had time. Yet she had time now. Tavarra darted to the side and ran for the shelter. Not only did she need to retrieve a weapon, but she wanted to get her necklace and find her boots, then kill this thing before he wreaked havoc on anyone else, the way they did on the bats. Bats. Eza was most likely one of the last, if not, *the last*. Of all the years Tavarra swam to shore as a sea dweller, and the seven years she had been on land, she hadn't seen any sign of another.

Before she hit the first of the steps leading into the shelter, two forceful arms pulled her back, holding her tightly. "Do not move. I will not hurt you." Tavarra didn't listen, but the creature was too strong, and she wasn't much competition in her current state. Yet if he wanted to kill her, he could have done it already, could have snapped her neck, too.

"Let go, you fool!" Tavarra shouted, digging inside for whatever strength she could find. She quickly maneuvered her upper body as he listened, his arms slacking. It was enough to throw him back, his left side hitting the ground with a heavy clunk.

She peered down at herself for a minute, not knowing

where the strength came from, just like from when she broke the manacle that was still dangling from her wrist. Shaking wishful thinking away, she stared at the jovkin as he brushed off the dirt from his legs and stood. She wanted to rip off his arms and step on them like twigs. "Don't touch me again."

The jovkin nodded.

She didn't trust him, not in the least, but she needed to get her boots and scavenge a few things. "I'm going inside, and if you follow me, you're dead. Understand?" He would be dead anyway when she came out with weapons.

Again, the jovkin nodded.

Not taking her eyes off him as she entered the shelter, Tavarra went straight back into the room where Ian had kept her. All her things were tucked in the corner next to the dresser. Only her necklace was on the table—she grabbed it and placed it on the bed. Her boots had seen better days, but she shoved them on after changing into another set of clothes from her bag. *These ones can stay here and rot.* After tucking her new daggers at her waist, she finally unlocked and took off the manacle from her wrist, not knowing why she hadn't done that first.

But she did know why, because she'd had hope. Slowly, she moved to the head of the bed and gripped the wood in both hands. Closing her eyes, she struggled to crack it in half. It didn't budge, and she let go then dropped to the bed.

It was all just hopeful thinking, but she couldn't let it get to her. After all, she had wanted the curse gone, right? Before any tears could bloom to life, she gathered her emotions and put on a strong face, then placed her necklace back around her throat. She shouldered her pack and took some of the other weapons and leftover food she found in the dining area. A part of her screamed that she had killed Ian's partner. *No, Tavarra, not you, your monster did it. The monster is gone. Besides, the man had come to hunt you down first, and Ian held you hostage without a monster being unleashed.* Ian was dead now, not because of her, but because of the jovkin outside. Did he expect a thank you for that?

No, the fucker needs to be dead, like the rest of them.

When she opened the door, the jovkin still stood there, hadn't even budged from his spot. Tavarra lunged at him, but she was weighed down by the pack and the sword at her hip that she wasn't used to. He twisted away from her, a limber giant, yet not much taller than her.

Using a snake-like movement, he managed to grab her wrists when she flew at him once more. "Do not do that again," he said almost gently, releasing his hold on her. "I am not trying to harm you."

Panting, heart on fire, her anger grew as she stared him down. He looked like every other jovkin. But as she breathed hard and peered more closely, his eyes were wider than some, nostrils smaller, ears sticking out a little farther.

An idea struck her then. Perhaps she could just kill him later. A life for a life—she could gift him that this one time. If the jovkin hadn't interrupted, she would be dead now. "Who are you? And why aren't you trying to rip me apart without question?"

"Not all of us are uncivil," he said, golden eyes flickering.

"Hmm." She didn't believe that as she readjusted her pack. "All right, well, I'm going to go now. If you follow me, I'll kill you."

Squeezing past the jovkin, Tavarra made sure not to touch him but kept an eye on his form until she was a good enough distance away. She wouldn't think about the buffoon ever again. Before she moved on past dips and over logs, she wiped the sweat from her forehead. The weapons, the pack, all of it, felt heavy, and she hated that because she'd never had a problem with things being too hard to carry when she'd had the curse.

Sucking it up, Tavarra followed the direction of the suns, the way the mountains were angled, and the sounds of trickling water. She would need to wash up first. Mr. Sivley's village wasn't that much farther—she could possibly make it before the suns set.

Behind her, the crunch of sticks and leaves reverberated, followed by heavy stomping. He was dead—so dead. She had warned his foolish ass. Holding up her dagger, she slowly turned around, finding the jovkin at the right distance for her to kill.

Tavarra hurled her dagger, perfectly … and the bastard drew up his hand, catching it *perfectly*.

"What are you *doing*?" she spat, pulling another from her waist.

"I do not … I do not have anywhere else to go at the moment." He paused, holding her dagger out toward her. "And I am not sure you do, either." She didn't make a move … yet.

Tavarra stared into the creature's golden eyes, waiting for a deceptive move as he stood there with her weapon. Slowly, she edged forward, another dagger ready, while she yanked her weapon from his hand.

"Aren't most of your kind wanderers?" she asked, holding up both blades. "I've never seen a cluster full of you. Just usually one roaming around, unless near peach trees, then possibly several, wherever their filth chooses to take them.

"And besides," Tavarra continued, "you don't want to be around me. I've eaten your kind for dinner. Straight to the bones."

His shoulders sagged in an oddly human way. "Then, if you must, kill and eat me. I do not care."

What? Something about his expression unnerved her, that he *wanted* her to kill him. Tavarra wouldn't satisfy his needs, wouldn't give the bastard what he desired. She turned and walked away. He followed. Not once did she look back again—she didn't need to hear his story. Everyone had one, and she was sick of them, sick of her own damn story.

Along the way, she washed up at a river, feeling much

better. Then she ate dried meat from Ian's cottage and plucked a couple pieces of fruit to place in her pack for later. The jovkin didn't eat any. *If he wanted some, he could have grabbed some—he has two hands, after all.* The journey remained silent and oddly comforting. She had never truly been alone until the last few weeks. There had always been Nezarra, Brice, or Eza, and for a bit of time, there was Perin.

Gripping the necklace at her throat, Tavarra closed her eyes for a moment while she walked—only a dull ache remained in her foot. Finally, she let the objects go. She *needed* to let go. Let *them* go.

A human heart bruised just as much as any heart, and she didn't know if she wanted to keep this one any longer.

For the remainder of the way, she ducked under tree limbs and watched forest life pass by. The jovkin didn't reach to eat any of that either.

One hand stayed at the sword at her hip, and the other rested on the dagger. She could throw a dagger easily, and she knew her aim would be true this time. Eza had taught her well.

Up ahead, past a waterfall, sat Mr. Sivley's village. The shelters were a mixture of ones being fully repaired and others dilapidated because of the volach attack years ago that Eza had told Tavarra about.

She turned to face the nuisance. "Here's what we're going to do … Jovkin."

"Vaden," he said softly, peering past her at the cluster of shelters.

Arching an eyebrow, Tavarra wrinkled her nose. "Excuse me? What was that gibberish?"

His golden eyes locked on hers. "My name is not Jovkin, it is Vaden."

She didn't give a rat's ass what his name was. He was *Jovkin*. "All right. I'm going to go into that village for a little while, and when I come back, you better be gone unless you truly do want a dagger in your heart."

Tavarra expected the jovkin—who she would not call by his true name—to follow her. But he didn't, and she was satisfied that he listened to her threat.

High above, the suns still glowed fiercely—she had made good timing. Enough time to bid a "hello" and "goodbye." Perhaps it was better for her not to relay the news about Eza, but from the short interaction Tavarra had with Mr. Sivley, he had cared about her friend and had even offered them both a place to stay.

A strange familiar sense hit her when she glanced toward the village, catching a glimpse of Mr. Sivley gardening in front of his shelter. Only this time, Eza wasn't there jolting ahead to meet him.

Tavarra paused for a moment, closing her eyes and gathering her emotions.

I'm here, even if you can't see me, Eza would have said.

"I really wish you were," Tavarra murmured, loosening her fists as she silently came upon Mr. Sivley. He must have been too consumed with gardening to hear her footsteps.

"Mr. Sivley?"

Whirling around, the man pressed a hand to his chest, scrambling to stand up. His eyes took a moment to focus on her as he ran a dirt-covered hand across his gray mustache. "You came back."

"For a moment."

He stared at her harder, squinting his dark eyes. "You look a bit different, only a fraction, though. You must have found what you were looking for."

"I did, yes." She tried to smile but couldn't bring herself to do so. "Thank you."

His gaze shifted past her shoulder. "Where's Eza?"

"That's what I came here to tell you. She didn't make it." Tavarra screamed inside her head over and over for him not to ask how it had happened because she wouldn't be able to explain it without breaking down.

"Oh, my dear girl." Mr. Sivley reached out a hand to comfort her but must have thought better of it when Tavarra backed up. The man seemed nice enough with his kind eyes and wrinkled skin, but she didn't want him touching her when it came to talking about Eza. It would only make her fall to pieces, and she didn't need that.

"Come in." He waved her on with the garden tool in his hand. "I can brew you some tea."

"No, no. I can't. I just … wanted you to know because she genuinely cared about you."

He smiled as water gathered in his eyes. "She was such a unique creature, wasn't she?"

"She was." Tavarra took a step away. "I really should be leaving."

"Are you sure I can't get you some tea? I can give you whatever you want to take with you."

She forced herself to smile because Eza would have wanted her to. "No, but thank you."

"If you ever need a place to stay, there are several old houses open."

"Possibly." Tavarra knew the word was false as soon as she said it—she wouldn't be back. "Goodbye." She walked away, hearing him wish her a safe journey. Those words did it. The tears came that time. One. Two. Three. Too many. So she took a deep breath, promising herself she would harden her emotions. She pulled back in what remaining water wanted to come after a few last sniffles, then inhaled the woodsy scent so characteristic of this part of Laith.

When the jovkin—Vaden—stepped out from behind a tree. She had almost forgotten about him.

Narrowing her eyes—which was hard for her not to do at anyone these days—Tavarra retrieved her dagger. "Why are you here? I told you to go."

He studied his hands, not looking at her. "I do not have anywhere else to go."

She closed her eyes and walked around him. "I don't have anywhere else to go, either, but here I am."

"You could have stayed there, in that village," Vaden said behind her.

"I could have, but it's not my home." Once again, she didn't have one of those. It took her long enough to figure out that Eza was her home, and now she was gone.

Tavarra's stomach rumbled, and she took an apple from her pack and bit into it. Again, the jovkin didn't ask for any, nor did she offer—she expected him to try and rip it from her hand, but he didn't. The jovkins loved fruit, especially peaches, but they also relished eating anything and everything living.

It was something that Tavarra used to be able to do, but she couldn't anymore with the curse gone. Only weapons now.

In the distance, the suns were beginning to set, and her movements came to a halt. She pressed her body up against a tree and drew in a panicked breath. This was going to be one of those nights where she wouldn't be able to control her anxious thoughts. Hurriedly, she sat down and pulled open her pack.

"What are you doing?" Vaden asked, kneeling beside her.

"Nothing!" Tavarra snapped. The chains rattled as she tugged them out. She couldn't even bring herself to care that a jovkin was standing right beside her, because she needed to be bound. After placing a manacle along one wrist, she looped the chain around the tree and put the shackle on her other one. She didn't fasten them, but she wanted to be prepared just in case the beast ever did decide to come out. But maybe she shouldn't since the jovkin kept lurking at her, clearly confused.

"It does not look like nothing to me," Vaden said, way too late.

Perhaps there was something she could say to make him go away. She wished she could bring herself to stab him, but his pitifulness made the thought seem almost cruel. Maybe there was a way to bring his inner beast to the surface. "There's a reason why Ian—the man whose neck you snapped—held me prisoner."

"I already knew who Ian was," he mumbled. "Why do you think I was there?"

That got her attention, her gaze shifting to his. "You *knew* him?"

Vaden pressed his back against the tree beside Tavarra's and slid down with his hand over his chest, as though he had been shot through the heart. "Yes. He murdered the female who I loved."

Loved? The jovkins don't *love*. "What do you mean?"

"Aubrey and I had come to Ian's after he left a letter for her near the peach trees, where we would still come to every so often after she left her home to be with me. From the note, it seemed as though Ian wanted to make amends with us for forcing her to leave. But when we arrived, Aubrey got caught in one of the traps. He came out with his bow and shot her right in front of me. I managed to escape with her body while he shot me several times in the back."

The tale was already strange. Why would Ian invite two jovkins to dinner? And Aubrey had once lived with Ian? "Yet, you live."

"She was his sister." He ground his jaw. "And he had set the trap on purpose."

Tavarra stilled, unable to figure out how to string words together for the longest time. "Wait, what? You were with a *human*?" As a sea dweller, she had loved Brice, but she had never heard of a jovkin and a human together. She wasn't exactly sure how that could work out, or if the parts would join together right, or if he even had a part hidden in there. The jovkins were always naked, just as she had been as a sea dweller, but she and Brice could never be together until she had legs. The male jovkins' appearance down there was more like armor surrounding their manhood, with a distinct bulge. She didn't want to look anymore.

"Yes, I met Aubrey in the forest where she would go almost daily to pick peaches. I thought she was the most beautiful thing I had ever seen. And one day, I finally handed her a peach."

"And what did she do?" Tavarra's interest piqued at this.

"She took the peach, of course." Vaden smiled as though trapped in the memory. Seeing a jovkin's lips pulled up that way—without sneering—was slightly unnerving. If this creature handed another human a piece of fruit, most would have run off screaming or taken out a weapon. Tavarra would have slit his throat. She wasn't sure why she hadn't done that to begin with.

Ian really was a bastard.

"Anyway, Aubrey was shunned by Ian and Les, and we discovered a new place to stay. When Ian left a bottled note near a peach tree, hoping for Aubrey to find it and come back with me, we should have known it was too good to be true. Her brother and his partner had tried to murder me numerous times. And now, I do not know how to go back to being just me anymore."

"Here's my advice—you just do it." She settled down into the dirt and shut her eyes. "That's all any of us can do."

Ten

Perin

Perin didn't wait for Lana—he couldn't. He left. Would she be mad? Probably. But he still hoped she decided to keep quiet to Rhona when his sister did come back … and if he didn't.

The sea would take him a few days to get to if he didn't stop too much except for rest at night.

Rain started to fall as he walked down a hill, the wet mud already making the slope slippery. He kept recalling the interaction with Lana, and how a scent wafted off her that made him hungry … for her.

As Perin leaped across a large puddle at the end of the hill, he grabbed a twisted branch to help swing him across. When he landed, he placed a hand to his chest to feel the beat of his heart. It was there—not faster, not softer, just the same old *thump-thump*.

"I'm not dead if there's a heartbeat. But I am something…" he whispered as the rain slowed, and he pushed past thorny vines and bright orange flowers. The shade perfectly matched a certain woman's hair.

He plucked one and brought it to his nose as he continued forward. There was a part of him that thought maybe his sense of smell was off, in the same way his tastebuds were, but the floral scent hit his nostrils. It smelled nothing like *her*. She had an odor that was more of the sea, fruit, and nature.

Thinking of her caused him to think of her werewolf. Tavarra had a curse for years and didn't give up. He had what could only be considered "Perin's Curse" for days, and he wanted it to end. Perhaps she was much stronger than him.

There were tales his village had passed down that he'd mentioned to Tavarra. Vampires, werewolves, *zombies*. And he'd avoided that last thought because, yes, he had died and come back to life, but not from being infected. It was because of some strange shit with the ground that some forgotten goddess had concocted. His heartbeat still functioned, his skin wasn't rotting, he could think and talk clearly, not gibberish or grunts. But he did enjoy fresh meat…

As though hearing his thoughts, his stomach cramped with a forceful blow. He pressed his palm to a branch and retrieved his dagger with his other hand. It had been a while since the jovkin meal, and he needed fresh meat again.

Letting go of the branch, he focused on the rustling sounds in the distance. Drogwais. Three scurried across, and he launched his dagger, striking a brown and white one down. Not quick enough for escape.

Perin picked up the furry creature and retrieved his dagger. He remembered Quil showing Rhona how to skin a drogwai so that there would be more meat to eat. As his nostrils flared, he didn't have the patience to sit and wait, so he bit straight in, fur and flesh and all.

He ate as he moved, and even after finishing the drogwai, the blood lingered on his mouth and fingers. It wasn't so much the blood he wanted, but the meat. He couldn't help but let his eyes flutter at the taste. However, something hadn't been right, the flesh didn't taste as exhilarating as the jovkin's. But he couldn't dwell on that.

The suns had already started to fall, and he would have to make camp soon. He didn't want to stop, not even when a river slid into view. He just wanted to hurry and get to the sea. But the smart thing to do was to come to a stop, so he unshouldered his pack and washed his face and arms.

Perin thought about starting a fire, but he just wanted to be alone in the darkness. He lay back and stared at the two silvery full moons and wondered at that moment if Tavarra was looking at them, too.

"Stop," Perin whispered to himself. He couldn't think about her, but that only left one place for his thoughts to turn to as he tried to sleep.

It was going to be time for the bonfire soon, and Perin couldn't find Rhona. He knew the wishes at the fire never came true for him, but maybe they could for her.

She was supposed to meet him at the edge of the village so they could pick fruit to bring to the fire, but he stood there alone. His tiny heart kicked up. Something was wrong. No matter what, she'd never failed to meet him before, even if she had run a little late a few times.

Stars lit up the sky as he made it to the middle of the village where people were feasting, talking, and throwing in logs to watch the flames of the fire trickle higher and higher. The crackling echoed in his ears as he searched the faces of everyone.

Belen stood at the front, and Thea stood not too far away from him. But Rhona was not there.

Maybe she didn't feel well? His breath caught in his throat. What if Belen had done something awful to her, more terrible than he'd ever done to either of them? The paranoid thoughts spiraled inside him as he rushed to her tent.

He passed home after home until he stopped in front of Rhona's tent. On the outside, paintings of what was supposed to be Neverland, with a picture of Peter Pan and his crew, adorned the fabric. He'd helped her with them earlier that day.

Perin lifted the curtain to the entrance. "Rhona?"

A small sniffle answered, and he brought up his lantern

into the darkness, lighting up the room.

"What's wrong?" he asked when his gaze met her reddened eyes. Her cat, Peter, was asleep in her arms.

"It's Peter," she said softly, not moving from her position.

"What's wrong?" Perin asked again, stepping inside and staring at the fluffy white cat. He'd helped Rhona pick Peter out months ago from one of the neighbor's litters. The kitten had come straight toward Perin before deciding he would be a better fit for Rhona. He would have never taken the cat home, anyway. Not with Belen.

"He's dead."

"What do you mean dead?" The cat only looked as if it were sleeping, but he would have already shot up his tiny head by now. Peter always darted for Perin right when he entered.

"I don't want to talk about it," she said, tears streaming down her face.

"It was him." Perin scooped up the lifeless kitten into his arms. "He made you do something you didn't want to do, didn't he?"

"Yes..." She nodded and pressed her bare feet to the ground.

"Come on, then. I'll help you bury Peter." He sighed.

They walked in silence while Rhona guided them with the lantern until they reached the field. Colorful flowers abounded, and trees seemed to be in dancing forms. But everything appeared shadowed at night under the light of the moons.

"Do you want me to dig?" he asked when they came to a stop.

"I can do it." Her tears had gone away, replaced by a new emotion. With her garden shovel, she began to unearth the ground.

After they covered Peter, Perin turned to Rhona. "Do you want me to get you a new kitten?"

"No, I don't want a pet ever again."

That small change in Rhona caused by Belen only made Perin's hatred for his father intensify.

Perin's eyes bolted open, and he scrambled to his feet, sword in hand, until he realized he'd only been dreaming. Belen was gone, but the memories still haunted him. He should have tried to do more, but he and Rhona had both been raised to believe they were nothing. However, Perin was the only one who actually believed it.

Gathering his pack and refilling his canteen after finishing his water, Perin started for the sea. He had a new plan until he reached his destination, and that was to eat as much fresh meat from non-human creatures as he could.

His solution was short-lived because he'd only been able to scavenge mice and small birds. So the next day was repetitive in his routine—walk, eat meat, walk, eat meat. Neither fulfilled him, but his stomach ached less.

When there wasn't any life he could eat, Perin had to settle for his dried meat and fruit. That morning, he woke with his stomach burning, and he held back a shout when he almost toppled over as he stood.

As he moved on, he didn't even bother with the dried meat or the fruit, because it was pointless if they weren't doing anything for his hunger. The water seemed to help dull his stomach for a little bit, as though plumping it up. So he drank from his canteen, trying not to finish it off.

From the open spaces in between the trees, relief swam through him as he captured the glistening tops of the sea waves dancing to and fro.

As his feet planted in the sand, he stared out at the water, listening to the beautiful clashing sounds. *Fuck.* How long would it take for him to make it across? There was no way he could swim across it. His gaze swept to the side, catching on a line of boats.

His lips tilted upward. "Maybe today will be a lucky one."

Tied to a long wooden pier, the boats buoyed up and down

against the sea's lithe movements. The pier sat abandoned, as though agreeing with his chance.

Perin didn't have his cloak to conceal his appearance, so he hurried as quickly as he could against the tedious sand. His boots *thump-thumped* over the wooden pier, and he headed for the first boat he saw with large, white triangular sails. It most likely held at least one small room buried beneath the deck.

Just as his hands touched the rope that was tied horribly to begin with, a man appeared from below the deck. "Excuse me?" he bellowed. The man had a deeply reddened face from too much sun and a beefy build that could possibly challenge him—if he was as quick as Perin.

The man hopped down in front of him, and Perin straightened but didn't move back. "Was just going to borrow the boat for a bit." Perin shrugged with nonchalance.

"The fuck you are!" The man withdrew the sword at his hip.

"The fuck I am." Perin unsheathed his weapon. "Or would you prefer I borrow one of your friends' boats? That could be another option." He wasn't good at asking for things nicely, but that was the best he could do.

"You're not taking anything from here, outsider." With a growl, the man charged forward, swinging his sword at Perin.

Past the pier and beyond the trees, he knew this man came from a village like Belen's, where the people were so self-absorbed that they hated everyone except themselves. He had never understood the concept.

Perin easily dodged the stranger's slow movements. He didn't want to kill the gent, but he might have to. After all, the man made the first move, not him.

With too heavy footing, the man lunged for Perin once more. Perin raised his sword and shoved the man back. "I don't think you want to play this game with me. I'll win."

Fishing out something from his waist, the man tugged out a dagger and threw it in response. Perin shifted out of the way, but it nicked his bicep as it flew past, leaving a sharp sting in its wake. "So, you want to play dirty then?"

For the third time, the man shot forward at Perin, like an idiot. Holding up his sword, Perin moved out of the way, then he spun and brought it down. Instead of the man clacking his sword against his as he'd expected, the idiot ran forward, impaling himself on Perin's weapon.

There was a gasp from the man, then only silence.

Rolling his eyes at the pinkened sky, Perin pulled out his sword—now coated in the man's blood. "This could have been such a simple chit-chat," he said as the corpse slumped to the wooden pier. "Now look what you've done." People always tended to let their emotions take over when they didn't have to. This fool—as Tavarra would say—was one of them.

He stared down at the man and searched around to see if anyone else was around, then let out a sigh.

The boat now sat in front of Perin, ready for him to set sail. But he stood frozen when a metallic scent invaded his nostrils, permeating the air. Fresh flesh.

Shaking his head, Perin took a step forward, stopped, and turned back around to peer down at the man. His stomach ached, and the idiot *was* dead. What harm would it do? Was it really so different than eating a dead jovkin? Hell yes, it was.

Should I? Or should I not? Should I? Or should I not?

A thought crossed his mind about going across the sea with only dried meat and fruit in his pack. If Rhona was the one going through this, what would he tell her to do? The answer would be for her to eat. Though he wasted precious moments weighing his options, Perin already knew what his best and final choice would be. Disgusted with himself, he knelt beside the stranger and plunged his dagger into the man's stomach, ripping the flesh apart.

Eleven

Tavarra

"Tell me your story," Vaden said. "I don't even know your name."

"It's probably better we keep it that way."

Tavarra was good at finding strays. Bryce. Eza. Perin ... Vaden. They had been resting at the same spot for several days—she hadn't felt like moving anywhere else. And she hated to admit it, but that frightened her. It wasn't because of fear at what else lay out there—another bastard ready to strap her to a bed—or worse? Rather, she wasn't sure where to go next. Even if she had something specific to search for like the Stone of Desire, that would have at least been *something*.

Vaden blew out a puff of air. "At least tell me your name."

She could give him that after he killed Ian and opened up about Aubrey. "Fine. It's Tavarra."

"Tavarra," Vaden repeated. "It rolls right off the tongue, does it not?" He rolled a part of her name, making it sound foreign, but not awful.

"I suppose the way you say it, it does." Tavarra stood from the ground, coming up with a decision. She would travel to the one place where she could think and possibly figure out where to go from there.

"Where are we going now, Tavarra?" Vaden lengthened his spine and stretched his arms while releasing the loudest of yawns.

She halted mid-reach for her pack and slowly turned to face him. "*We* are not going anywhere—*I* am going to the sea to visit."

"You come from the water, then?"

"No!" She snapped out the word too quickly. "Why would you ask that?"

Not caring that she could bite off his fingers, he lifted a lock of her tangerine hair, then dropped it. "The color of your hair is not one of humans, and the way you move your arms and hands is more of a lyrical sway."

"What are you talking about, Jovkin?"

"From what I know about you thus far, you would not go to visit the sea unless you were a part of it," Vaden said so calmly and matter-of-factly that she couldn't find a response. So she bit the inside of her cheek as hard as she could, gathered her things, and walked away. The jovkin didn't seem the least bit bothered by the anger rolling off her in fiery waves as he followed her.

As they wandered through the dense forest, Vaden was smart enough to keep quiet. Despite drinking water on the way, Tavarra remained thirsty because of the heat. She was tired of carrying the heavy pack, tired of the sword thumping against her leg that she hadn't even used. Tired in general.

Her thoughts went back to the damn sea. Perhaps she should just go somewhere else. What was she planning to do after visiting the sea? Where would she go? Roam around alone? Go back to Rhona's? Or Mr. Sivley's? The first option, she decided. But to do that, she would have to somehow get rid of Vaden when they got to the ocean. Most likely when he fell asleep, so he wouldn't try and follow.

A rustling stirred in the flowered bush to her right. She reached for a dagger as a furry black rabbit darted by.

"Hungry?" Vaden asked, his eyes never leaving the small creature.

"Yeah." She pulled out her dagger, but the jovkin zipped by her, hunching over with speed and precision, leaving Tavarra no time to breathe as she watched. He raised his hand and brought it down, tearing the head clean from the body in one smooth fatal swipe.

Tavarra's eyes widened at the predatory skills of the jovkin. As a cursed creature, she had been able to do things like that once. A fraction of a smile crossed her face, impressed.

She waited for him to dig right into the body or the head of the rabbit. But instead, he said, "Build a fire?"

"You don't eat it raw?" she asked, already gathering loose sticks from the leaf-covered ground and making a small pile.

Sticking out his blackened tongue in disgust, Vaden shuddered. "Never."

"Hmm, you are a very strange jovkin indeed."

"Perhaps you should not lump us all together."

All she could do was blink at him, then blink again. She turned away with her chest tightening, the thought lingering in her head. Was she feeling guilty?

She had lumped the human males together time and time again, and she had done the same thing with the jovkins regardless of their sex. Would she want anyone to think that sea dwellers or human females were all the same? No, she would not. She would claw whoever believed that.

"Listen, Jovkin," Tavarra started, pursing her lips, "if you go with me to the sea and make one wrong move, I'll stab you in the chest and eat your heart raw."

The jovkin's flat nose crinkled upward. "That does *not* sound like a tasty delicacy."

Rolling her eyes, Tavarra ripped the rabbit body from his hand. "Do you know how to get a fire going?"

"Yes."

"Then help me cook." She sat down, and he fell to his knees beside her, reaching for a stick to use.

Vaden was far superior than her at starting a fire, but she wouldn't admit that out loud. He showed efficiency when he gathered better leaves and branches to add to her pathetic pile, then he rubbed his fingers up and down one of the twigs, blowing out quick breaths as a flicker of orange flame and smoke rose skyward. Placing the rabbit on the end of a sharp stick, she rotated the meat above the fire, letting the smoky scent fill her nostrils.

With her dagger, she split the meat in half, keeping the larger portion for herself. "You're right," she murmured, not making eye contact. "I was from the sea."

He glanced over at her, grease covering his lips. "Hmm?"

"I *said*, you were right." She tapped one of the rabbit bones against the heel of her boot before tossing it away. "I was born in the sea, and I was not human. I was a sea dweller."

"Then how did you become human?" His golden eyes flickered as he searched for an answer while scanning her face. He wouldn't find one there.

"That's all I'm willing to share for now."

"All right." He nodded and changed the subject. "I miss Aubrey..." The emotion in his voice sounded distraught, so unlike any other jovkin she had ever seen.

"I'm sure you always will." Tavarra still missed Nezarra's laugh, even though years had passed without hearing it. She also missed Eza's humor and Perin's stubbornness.

After eating, they trekked through the forest in silence until night fell. About a half day's journey remained, and Tavarra's muscles ached from walking for so long. With a relieved sigh at the rest awaiting her, she dropped to the ground and pulled out the shackles from her pack.

"Would you prefer to chain me to the tree?" Vaden asked, running a hand over his wrist.

She stared hard at the jovkin, growing suspicious. "Are

you sure you weren't anything else? Were you cursed as a jovkin? Once a human?"

"No, I've always just been me." He paused. "I had a great mother. She raised me differently, and yes, she was a jovkin, too."

As she peered at the large moons, her heart sped up. It was another night where she needed to be confined to the tree. Staring at his wrists, she said, "You don't need to be chained." Then Tavarra latched herself to the trunk and turned away from Vaden. Moments slipped by until a whisper passed her lips—she didn't even know if he could hear her. "I've lost people, too. My sister has been gone for years, and that's how I know you'll never stop missing Aubrey."

—|—

Tavarra shot through the surface of the water, near the small chunk of land in the center of the sea. There she found a sprite with golden wings fluttering beneath the stars.

"What are you doing out here, sea dweller?" the sprite asked.

"Trying to be something other than a sea dweller." She let her body float on its back, gazing up at the night sky, wishing her tail could be split into two.

The sprite flew nearer until she was incredibly close to Tavarra's face. "You do know there's a way."

"You talk lies." Sprites were known to be little tricksters at times, but their games tended to focus on stealing and manipulation.

"When the moons are at their fullest, you can remove your tail and discover legs hidden beneath." The sprite giggled and darted away, calling over her shoulder, "But you must return within one full day."

Drenched in sweat, Tavarra shot up and was pulled back

by the clanking of her chains. Everyone would still be alive if she had stayed beneath the sea. *Everyone.* She had known sprites were tricksters and had guessed it chose not to tell her the full tale. Nezarra had warned her, as well.

The morning light rose from behind the mountains in the distance, and Tavarra unlocked the chains. She stared down and rubbed the pinkened scars on her wrists, from all those nights she had jerked the shackles as the beast.

"Look what I got for us," Vaden said from behind, pulling her out of the reverie. Whirling around, she found the jovkin holding two fruits, one in each hand. *Peaches.*

Tavarra's heart accelerated—her chest was finding it so hard to draw in any air. She knocked the fruit from his hands and bared her teeth as she growled, "Get those *things* away from me."

Vaden's body froze, and he looked as if he didn't know what to say, too scared to move to pick up the fruit. "You do not like peaches..."

"I did like peaches once, but I don't anymore."

He tilted his head to the side. "Because they relate to something bad."

"Very bad." She dropped to her knees and pressed her hands to her head, holding back the tears that wanted to fall.

"Make me understand," he said, kneeling beside her but keeping a respectful distance, as if guessing it was what she most needed at that moment.

Tavarra didn't know why she decided to unravel her secrets, maybe because Eza wasn't there, and she was so used to telling someone everything. She couldn't hold it in anymore. None of it. Not about the curse she'd had, not about her sister, not about Eza, and not about Perin. And she managed to do it all without shedding a single tear.

When she finished, he nodded in understanding. "Then I shall not eat peaches, either."

"No, that's not what I meant when I knocked the fruit from

your hands," she said. "*I* can't eat them, but *you* can."

With his barefoot, he kicked the fruit farther away from him. "Peaches have led to deaths upon deaths. The bats are a special creature."

"I wish there were more. I hope Eza wasn't the last."

He stared ahead, crinkling his brow in consternation like he wanted to say something, then his gaze fell to the peaches. "Perhaps we can eat pears instead?"

She gave a small nod. "I'd like that."

They took the pears from her pack and hiked down a rocky path, leading to a place she had certainly been before. The village where her once beloved—Brice—most likely still lived. There used to be a desperate urge inside her to burn it all down, but now only indifference lingered.

She looked away from the different sizes of shelters and focused on the jovkin. "Have you ever been to the sea, Vaden?"

"You called me by *name*?" he said as though he couldn't believe it.

"I figured I wouldn't want you to call me 'human' the whole journey."

He smiled. "No, Tavarra, I have not been to the sea."

"Well, there's a first for everything." She shrugged and pushed branches out of the way until the sand became visible. The sounds of the sea rushed straight toward her, so familiar— as if the waves were bidding her a welcome back. As though she was always welcome there, no matter how long she chose to stay away.

When she stepped out onto the sand, Tavarra breathed in the salty air. She focused on the waves as she walked until she came upon boats weighted in place.

"What is that?" Vaden asked.

"What is what?" Following his pointed finger, she came to an abrupt halt. In the distance, down the pier, there was movement. "It looks like a man … eating someone."

She pushed her hand out to stop Vaden from heading toward the pier. "Stay here," she demanded and took off in a hard sprint.

She inched closer and closer to the man. Blood pooled out against the wooden boards, and he was certainly eating another person. "What the fuck?" Tavarra dropped her things and took out a dagger.

Did some humans do this to each other? As if in answer, the man turned around, and she immediately took a step back in shock, dropping the dagger. She recognized everything about him, but the body of the real man was buried in a meadow far away, not whatever *this* was.

"*What* are you?" She didn't wait for his reply as she took out her second dagger and lunged for him.

Twelve

Tavarra

Tavarra's heart struck her ribcage with something more cutthroat than hatred as she rushed at the human male. The *imposter*. The short brown hair, the bright blue irises, the strong jaw, straight nose—the *blood* all over his face, dripping down his chin. That was *not* Perin. She didn't know *what* it was, but it was not the man she had gotten to know. He was dead.

Her body made contact with the human, pushing him back to the floor of the pier, right as his eyes widened. But he didn't try to block her or fight back, as if he was as surprised as she was. Tavarra pounced down on him, placing the dagger directly at his throat. Just a little harder, and there would be even more blood filling up the space between them. This time, his.

"Who are you?" she shouted in his face, warm spittle spraying his cheek. "*What* are you?"

In response, the imposter closed his eyes and took a breath. "Are you going to release the blade from my throat first, Tavarra? You choked me once with your bare hand. Now a blade? What's next?"

Everything in her body stopped—her lungs, her

movements, her blinking—all except for her heartbeat, which she couldn't control, or it would have been at her mercy, too. When the cloud over her thoughts lifted away, she leaped from this imposter as if he had scalded her. "How do you know that? How do you know my name?" She should have just sliced his throat instead of trying to listen to whatever foolish words poured out from his bloody lips.

"Because it's me. Perin."

His last moments flashed in her mind—at the field, Rhona's mother had slammed the blade into his stomach. Tavarra had killed the woman for what she had done, then fallen beside Perin. She remembered holding her hand against his stomach to stop the bleeding. His words to her, words she had chosen to forget. *The night in the forest, when we danced under the moonlight, I should have kissed you then, too. A thousand times and more.* Moments later his breathing had stopped, and she had carried his limp body to his meadow, the one he had promised to take her to, the one that she took him to instead—dead. Buried. He was underground in that meadow, not here.

"Liar!" Tavarra's gaze fell to the dead body beside the imposter, the torn-out stomach, the stench of metal permeating the air, the crimson that was now coating her palms. "Perin's gone. I saw him die," she growled and pointed toward him. "Whatever you are, it's not him."

The man wiped the blood as best as he could from his hands—which wasn't much at all—against the planks and stood. "I know this looks fucked, and if I got embarrassed in the slightest, I would be the color of a red apple at its ripest and try to hide somewhere. But I don't. This is more of an 'I wish you had come sooner than later' type of situation."

"What is happening here?" Her anger was drifting into one of confusion.

"I'm in a bit of an extremely odd situation, sort of what you had going on with your curse. So if it's possible, I'm going to take this boat now, as originally planned, before this idiot impaled himself on my sword. I need to figure my shit out, then I'll come back here and meet you in a few weeks. How does that sound?"

Tavarra's lips parted, her right brow arching up as high as it would go before she roared, "How does that *sound*, fucker? What are you rambling on about?"

He lifted his pack and placed it around his shoulder. "You were a bit calmer when we first met. I think I preferred fool over fucker."

"Tell me exactly what's going on, or I swear on Laith itself that I will pierce you straight through the heart."

"You would have done that already if you truly believed I wasn't Perin," he said, and she could have sworn it was meant to be a jest, but she wasn't laughing.

Could it really be? "How then? *How*?"

"Remember in Lana's spare room when we had a discussion, and you mentioned that things stay dead in Laith?"

All the dead things I've seen here have stayed dead, and no one lives forever. "Yes?" Her voice came out a bit shaky.

"We now know that things may not always stay dead here," he said, lifting his shirt to reveal a jagged scab on his stomach. "I woke up buried underground in the meadow and crawled my way out. I hoped you and Rhona might have been at the Stone of Desire, but too much time had passed. Somehow, I roused the Stone."

"You said the Stone doesn't answer to humans any longer."

"It doesn't. Apparently, the Goddess who created Laith made the meadow special, and it's a place in which the dead can be awakened if it so chooses."

Their conversation. Vampires… Werewolves… "Zombie…" Tavarra murmured. She knew then that this was Perin—she knew it with her whole heart.

"You remember." Perin's lips tilted up a notch. His gaze

then shifted to the side, and a scowl crossed his face as he peered over Tavarra's shoulder. He unsheathed his sword and shouted, "Watch out!"

"Stay away from her!" a voice barked, one Tavarra had forgotten was around. Vaden. She had told him to stay where he was. She should have known he wouldn't listen because he hadn't all along.

Closing her eyes for a brief moment, she knew what Perin was seeing. A jovkin—the way she had. Tavarra moved in front of Perin, blocking his path. "Stop, he's … fine. The nuisance isn't a problem."

Perin stared at her as though she had lost her mind. And maybe she had. He didn't lower his blade as he shifted around her. "If you look behind me," he spat to Vaden, "there was an altercation earlier with another. Might not want to proceed much farther, because the ground is where you'll end up."

Tavarra clamped a hand on Perin's shoulder, tugging him back. "I can't believe I'm saying this, but don't. He's … he helped me along the way."

With eyes the widest she had ever seen on Perin, he whirled around. "I'm sorry, w*hat*?"

"I don't know what he is… A friend? No, that wouldn't be right, because I haven't known him that long. Helper?" Tavarra cringed. She hadn't known Perin terribly long either but she considered him a friend, so maybe that was what Vaden was becoming. "Perhaps I do mean friend."

The jovkin stepped forward, the intensity from earlier had left his face and body. "My name is Vaden."

"Come any closer, and you'll lose that head, *Vaden*." In contrast, Perin's intensity still radiated off him.

"All right"—Vaden held up his hands—"not the kindest of humans."

Tavarra looked around and noticed something was missing, or more so, *someone*. "Just let me finish this conversation, Vaden." She focused on Perin. "Have you told

Rhona? Where is she?”

“I can’t tell her.” Perin sighed. “But I did go to the village and talked to Lana to make sure my sister was fine.”

“I don’t understand. Why can’t you tell her?” Rhona needed to know—she deserved to.

“Because,” Perin began, “I didn’t get to finish the whole story. There’s this ‘magical’ lavender liquid the Stone needs for me to bring back. If that doesn’t happen, then I can’t be around her.” He flicked his gaze to the dead body. “You see what I mean?”

Tavarra followed his gaze and peered down at the cut-open body of the dead man. “It’s me here. I’m used to seeing and finding dead bodies, but what I’m not used to is one coming back to life and walking around as if they hadn’t died already.” She paused and pinched the bridge of her nose. “But your sister would want to know that you’re alive, and she could help you.”

“It’s better this way.”

“You always did think you knew better than everyone else, didn’t you?” A flame inside her ignited—growing brighter and higher—as she thought about him having Rhona knock her out with her ability. Tavarra wished she had her old strength, so she could shove his ass to the ground. She pushed at his chest anyway, and he shot backward, falling hard on his tailbone. Something was off again.

“You know I couldn’t have you go in there with my father,” he said, his frown softening. “Are you sure you’re human?”

“But you didn’t let me choose!” Tavarra screamed, pointing at her chest. “And, of course, I’m human, or I would have lifted your body and thrown it into the water!”

“I didn’t let you choose because you would have chosen to do the wrong thing!” He got to his feet, only a hair’s breadth away from her face.

“You—”

"I what?"

"You fool!"

"Here's what you're going to do." He was the first to step back, and she felt victorious. "You're going to drop this Vaden character off somewhere, then go back to the village and find Lana. Rhona and Quil are off having a tea party somewhere for another week." Turning around as if the conversation was over, he unlatched the rope to the boat.

"No," she seethed, not remembering this man being so insufferable.

"Come on, Tavarra," Vaden said. "Maybe we should go somewhere else."

Perin shot a hard glance to Vaden that would make most quake with fear, then he turned to Tavarra. "Look, I have too much going on. One includes me eating creatures' raw meat, like the dead body before you. I don't want to slip up around you."

He didn't want to eat her…

Rotating his shoulder, Perin spun around, and in one swing, he decapitated the head from the half-eaten body. Then he knelt and started to scrub the blood from his arms and face.

"Why did you do that?" she asked.

"In the tales about zombies, the dead that was eaten who still had their brain or head intact had a chance of coming back to wreak havoc. Just in case, I need to be sure he stays dead."

That made sense, but where was he even headed? "Where are you taking the boat to, exactly?"

"The Stone told me to go straight to the other side. A place known as Kova."

A chill ran up her spine as memories, that had remained dormant for years and were now dredged up, spun inside her. That wasn't a place for him to go, or any other human for that matter. They never returned.

"You can't go there!" She hurried to his side. "If you thought anything over here was dangerous, that place will tear you to shreds."

He shook his head. "I have no choice. You hated your curse, so you can't expect me to accept or relish in mine."

She wanted to disagree with those words and tell him that he was being a fool, but she couldn't. More than anything, she knew what it was like to hate what you were. "Then I'm going with you. From my time as a sea dweller, I know it will take a few days since traveling by boat is slower than by tail."

"And me," Vaden interrupted, already carrying her pack and weapons.

"No," Perin said.

"Come on, Vaden, our journey is going on a new course." Tavarra ignored him and hopped on the boat to a place she never thought she would visit again.

Thirteen

Perin

She was here... Beautiful, haughty, and stubborn Tavarra.

More stubborn than ever, but that was why he liked her. And that was why he needed to keep away from her.

Then there was this jovkin—Vaden. Why was he even here? Perin didn't have a problem with jovkins in particular, but all the ones he'd encountered wanted to fight to the death. And all had died by his blade … except for one. That creature which had perished and been ripped apart by Tavarra. He trusted her judgment—for the most part. After all, she'd just hopped into his boat even though she'd found him eating a man. But he supposed this jovkin could live … for now. It could very well not be the wisest of choices, and things would change quickly if the creature's actions proved otherwise deadly.

Perin watched as Vaden fished up the anchor.

Tavarra cocked her head his way and grabbed the helm of the boat. "You might want to come on board unless you're choosing to stay behind."

Despite thinking she should be the one staying behind, he jumped onto the deck, just as the boat pulled away from the dock to sail. "I told you no," he said, rising from his crouched position to stand. "I'm a risk."

"Grab the helm, Vaden, and move it to the right until the ship is angled with the suns." She stepped away toward the sails and tugged at the ropes, focusing on Perin. "You didn't seem to care too much about your own safety when I was a beast. You told me to keep myself unchained, remember?"

Shackles. He thought of something then that could possibly work for the time being. "Do you still have your chains?"

Tavarra finished looping the rope around a pole and placed her hands on her hips. "I do, and what of it?"

She knew what. "And I bet you're still chaining yourself, aren't you?"

Crossing her arms, Tavarra narrowed her eyes at him. He figured she still was because, even on nights when she wasn't the beast, she would do it. He'd seen her werewolf several times, and as monstrous as it could be, it was a true thing of beauty with elongated fangs, tangerine fur, and a ferocious roar meant to draw in dread from anything. There was a time when he could have wound up her prey, but he'd trusted his skills and lack of fear.

"I'd take that as a yes." Perin reached forward and took a few steps against the swaying deck. "Give them to me."

"No." She walked away from him. She *walked* away.

Frustration bubbled throughout his blood, and he followed her. "Instead of shackling yourself, I want you to chain me below deck until we reach the other side." It would be the safest option for all of them.

"Sorry, nope." Tavarra placed her hands on top of a large wooden barrel and peered inside. She dipped two fingers in and brought the clear liquid to her lips, changing the subject. "Looks like we don't have to conserve our water. This bucket has gathered plenty of rain."

"*Tavarra.*"

"I think she gave you her answer," Vaden said with an

apologetic expression.

Tavarra handed the jovkin her pack. "Vaden, can you make sure Perin doesn't try to do anything stupid while I take over the helm?"

With a shrug, Vaden placed her pack around his shoulders. "Of course."

Perin wanted to chop off the jovkin's fingers at that point, just one, but he inhaled and blew out a heavy breath and stepped away. He could easily take the pack if he wanted to, but he wasn't one to just take things.

"Okay, I see how it's going to be here. I'm going to go below deck for now." Turning around and searching the floor for the opening, Perin found the rectangular door. He lifted the metal ring to the creaking lid and traveled down the steps of the ladder. The boat rocked back and forth as he walked across the wooden floor, sailing onward.

A musty smell filled the room, as though it hadn't been used in a while. There wasn't much in there besides a blanketed mattress, two lanterns, a couple of books, a quill, and a stack of paper. To his right, a small square window let a minimal amount of daylight filter in.

Perin unstrapped his sword and took a seat on the pallet against the wall, pulling his knees to his chest. It was a sad attempt at relaxing physically but unfortunately did nothing for his wound-up thoughts.

Tavarra had said that it would only take a couple of days for them to make it to Kova. Could he survive the hunger and the pain until then? What had he done? He'd *eaten* someone, and he hated his actions, but like with the jovkin, the body would have just been left to rot otherwise. He pressed the heels of his hands against his eyelids, trying to take away seeing the color red, but it was still there.

The ladder creaked, signaling someone was on their way down. He jerked up his head to find Tavarra coming to a stop in front of him. "I thought I'd find you here."

"You knew I came this way," he said, looking out the window instead of at her. All he could see was light, not much to distract him from *wanting* to turn back and stare at her.

"That is true."

"You trust that jovkin up there with the helm?" Where else could Vaden go? Turn around and go back to shore, or set sail left or right?

"Frankly, I do." Tavarra absently grabbed something at her throat. "More than you. You broke that."

"You know I had to do it. Eza would have wanted me to."

She released the necklace, holding up her finger. "Don't you dare bring her name into this. The least you can do is say you're sorry." He caught a glimpse of his mother's ring that he'd given her and a shell that must have been Eza's gift, dangling from the necklace. His chest locked up—he'd given her that ring to let her know that he cared. The ring was his mother's, a woman he hadn't known, but it held hope. Hope that if his mother had lived, maybe his father would have been a better man. Hope that Perin could be better than his father.

"Why say something that's a lie? You don't want me to lie to you, so I'm not."

She gritted her teeth, tightening her fists. "*You…*"

"Tell me what happened with Rhona. Why did you split with her after going to the Stone?"

"Only if you tell me your story first."

"That again?" He shook his head. "I already told you what happened before you stole your passage aboard this boat. Now it's your turn."

"Fine. After we buried your body, Rhona took me to the Stone of Desire. I-I didn't want to, at first. I thought it would be pointless because Eza had died. And you … never mind. Anyway, the Stone changed me into a human, as you can see."

Even though Tavarra was still beautiful now as a human, she was just as much so before, even as the werewolf.

"Then what?" Perin asked, meeting her dark brown eyes.

"Then I couldn't go back to the village," she said, voice even. "It wasn't home. Nothing is anymore."

No matter that Tavarra had told him it wasn't his fault that Eza had been killed, he still felt he could have prevented it.

"So tell me, how did you get mixed up with a jovkin?"

With a sigh, Tavarra dropped down on the mattress and sat a little farther from him. "I picked a fight with another jovkin and stormed away, then I got caught in a human male's trap. The male tied me to a bed and kept me hostage because, as the beast, I murdered his partner. After several days passed, I escaped and he almost killed me, but Vaden saved my life."

Held her hostage to a bed... Perin straightened and reached for his dagger. "Turn the boat around now. I'm going to kill his ass."

"Too late," she said. "Vaden did that already."

"Did the man..." He couldn't finish that sentence.

"No. He would have been cut into pieces if he'd done that. But it did seem the man killed Vaden's love."

Perin relaxed a fraction, but fury still coursed in his veins. "A jovkin in love?"

Tavarra grinned, almost savagely. "Yes, with a *human* woman."

What the *fuck*... Perin pressed his hands to his temples. "I wasn't even sure jovkins mated. I mean, I know they have to since they are around, but..."

"I wasn't aware, either. Each time I've encountered one, I've killed them. At times, I specifically searched one out to release my emotions. Vaden's the first one I haven't killed."

He didn't blame her for her choices. He would have done the same thing. "Sometimes we're surprised by things we didn't know could be different."

"We are."

His choices lately were unpredictable, and the scent that radiated off her was pleasant, calming to him. But who knew how he would feel about it later when he grew hungry again.

"Listen, I need you to go back up. I'm starting to really not trust myself."

Tavarra moved from the mattress, but instead of heading up, she sat across from him on the floor against the wall. "I've got a better plan. How about I tell you a story this time?"

Perin furrowed his brow. "A story?"

"Yes, you fool, a story." She bit her lip and smiled. "You mentioned the Stone telling you about the Goddess, but you don't seem to know much about her. Lucky for you, I've heard her story. Aren't you the least bit curious?"

Damn it, he was. "No."

"Caught in a lie again." She tapped at her chin. "So, the tale begins with a female who loved so fiercely that she created Laith and everything in it. Two suns and two moons because she never wanted one to feel alone. This female was said to be an immortal—a goddess, Zada. But she fell in love with a spirit of Laith. This male wanted her power and immortality more than anything, so he found a way to curse her away by listening to the words from a sprite. However, things backfired for the male because the world and beings the Goddess had created weren't meant to be immortal without repercussions. In turn, he died, but the Goddess remained cursed and trapped from her home while parts of Laith became less beautiful."

"What was her curse?" Perin asked, adjusting himself to his side. "Where is she now?"

Tavarra shrugged. "No one knows."

"Then how was the story ever spun?"

"Who spun the story of *Little Red Riding Hood*?" she countered.

Tales were all made from something, but he didn't have an answer. "I don't know."

"I believe the story to be true, but as tales go from one to another, we both know how they can alter. But perhaps try wishing to the Goddess before you sleep."

"Did you?"

"For years. She never answered." Tavarra rose from the floor and glanced over her shoulder before heading up the steps. "Get some rest, Perin. I'll come back soon."

Closing his eyes, before drifting off, he did as Tavarra requested and asked the Goddess for help. She didn't answer him, either.

"I see how you choose to disobey me," Belen said. "You think me to be a monster, yet you are half of me, so wouldn't that make you one as well?"

Perin held his tongue because that would mean his sister was like Belen, and she was far from it.

"Clean up." Belen waved his hand in the air and turned around to leave. "You're still bleeding."

Three new wounds lined his chest. With an old wadded-up shirt, he placed the fabric to his skin to stop the crimson from trickling down. Sucking in a sharp breath, he tried to block out the stinging.

Strike one: You covered for Rhona.

Strike two: You asked about your mother again.

Strike three: You didn't clean your sword.

A new bonfire was beginning soon. He rubbed salve on his skin and gathered something to throw in the fire. He was tired of trying to find things to wish on that didn't come true. The Stone never answered him, the fire never answered him.

The fire was growing higher and higher, and he found Rhona tossing in something. He threw in his own item, wishing his father was dead.

He pulled Rhona to the side. "How about we run away?"

"Like Hansel and Gretel?" she asked, her blue eyes blinking several times.

"They didn't run away—the birds ate their bread crumbs. We could just go."

"I couldn't do that," she whispered, looking afraid that someone would hear them. "My ... my mother. She wouldn't go."

That part was true, but he knew the other part was because of the boy she met up with daily. It was a child's dream anyway, because Belen had a prism, and he would come after them. Even if they never left any bread crumbs to begin with.

She playfully shoved at his chest. "Go, have some fun."

The pain where she touched ignited, but he didn't let his emotions flicker. "How about you go dance? Belen isn't looking."

Rhona held out her palm. "Come?"

"No, I'll be your guard and whistle if he's near."

"Fine!" Rhona smiled and took off, running into the forest.

While she was gone, he swung his sword over and over, pretending it was his father's neck he'd struck.

Fourteen

Tavarra

Tavarra walked back up the ladder to the deck, finding Vaden still at the helm. The night was out, the moons bright, and the sea sparkling. She didn't feel the use for her chains that night—maybe eventually, she wouldn't need them at all.

Perin was alive. *Alive*! And she couldn't bring herself to fully grasp that perhaps she wasn't dreaming—she *knew* she wasn't. He was still the same suffering fool he had been before, but a fool who was alive!

"Your pack is beside the barrel if you need it," Vaden said, bringing a handful of water to his lips before moving to the edge of the ship to peer down at the sea.

"Not tonight. Besides, I have to watch over Perin in case his own beast arises." No one needed to steer the ship, since the ocean waves were driving the boat in the proper direction with the pads of their liquid fingers. Tavarra stopped beside him and stared down, too. Years had passed since she'd been out this far, and something inside her trembled. What if the ship sank at this moment? Would the sea swallow her back into its murky depths and never let her go? Even if the sea chose not to release her, she would be dead in the end because she no longer had gills.

"So that's Perin," Vaden said, a hint of an amused smile appearing.

No smile crossed Tavarra's face. "Yes, he's alive now, so I can truly be angry with him without feeling bad about it." Part of that was true, but she knew deep down in her heart, where the naïve dweller she once was lived, the other part wasn't.

"You know what I think?" He angled toward her and pressed his forearm against the edge. "I don't think you really want to be angry with him."

"Oh?" She scowled. "What would you know?"

"What I know is loss, like you." For the first time, Vaden placed his hand against hers and lifted her chin with the other. "If Aubrey came back from the dead, I would be over the moons, and I would show her how much I care."

"I bet Aubrey wasn't insufferable, though."

Vaden dropped his hand from her chin and gazed up at the stars. "At times, she very well could be, as could I. But I loved her all the more for it."

Tavarra let out a groan and sank onto the floor of the boat.

"So only a few days to make it across?"

"That's right." Tavarra remembered her time as a sea dweller and fearing nothing in the ocean. As a younger dweller, she had seen plenty of boats sail the sea, but most never ventured too far across. From the tales passed down, the sailors who had chosen to journey all the way to Kova never returned—whether the humans were alive or not, no one knew. Most likely, the majority of humans had stopped going because they had heard tales of their own, but that didn't stop them all.

Early on, Tavarra's parents had warned her and Nezarra about that side of Laith, known as Kova. *Only the wicked dwell there—only the wicked stay there.* Of course, Nezarra wouldn't go, nor would any other dweller, but Tavarra had … once.

Twelve-year-old Tavarra wasn't going to listen to her parents or her sister. They may be frightened of all things, but she wasn't. And she wasn't going to let the ocean stop her, either. Her home was beautiful, almost too much so. She wanted a challenge.

Tavarra fisted a pearl necklace she had strung for Nezarra—it had taken her so long to scavenge the perfectly round spheres. What if Kova had even better ones? How would she know unless she went?

Setting down the necklace, she knew what to do since her parents and sister were already asleep. Lately her father appeared sicker each day, and she knew his time was coming soon. She didn't want to live life without exploring everything.

With her blood pumping ferociously through her veins, Tavarra flicked her curled tail and traveled by the sea. She passed blinking blue and yellow lights, then more rainbows of color. Small purple and orange fish swirled around her as seaweed brushed her skin until finally, after swimming and more swimming, she left the safety of her territory.

Tavarra pressed her arms tightly at her sides as she shot past less colorful fish. Her eyesight was good, whether it was day or night. Yet as she drifted farther and farther out, the water became thicker, making it harder to see. Something felt off. As she looked side to side, she could see other creatures swimming, almost circling her with their hands clasped with one another. They looked like her kind but thinner, bonier, more skeletal with their fins mirroring that of a fish rather than her sea-horse-like tail. The mer.

One drew closer, with white hair floating around her head, sharp blackened teeth, dark eyes, and a hollow face. She brushed a pale hand across Tavarra's cheek, letting out a high-pitched giggle. "Come, little dweller. Stay for a bit?"

Holding back a scream, Tavarra broke through the dancing circle of predators. She knew if she agreed to follow the mer, she wouldn't ever return home. Flicking her fin, she dashed faster and faster, her heart accelerating through the darkness. The mer didn't follow, as though what lay ahead was more alarming than them. There were no sounds, no movement, only the ripple of the waves. Everything was becoming too dark. She wouldn't be able to search for pearls down here.

Quickly, she thrashed her tail and headed to the surface. She strained to see and became confused, uncertain if she was even going the right way.

Flipping her curled tail, she crashed through the surface and took a deep breath of the air above. The stars sparkled down on the sea, along with the crescent shapes of the moons. From her point of view, the top of the water looked the same as back home, no darker, and not obsidian.

Up ahead, the shore was close—she was almost there. With a bright smile, she cranked her arms through the water, keeping her head above as she went the rest of the way.

The remains of old boats spread out along the sand on the shore. So many ships—some large, others small, and even rafts. Most looked to be rotting and falling apart, not even the least bit whole.

When Tavarra came to the realization that her tail would prevent her from continuing on, she wanted to scream. Closing her eyes, she hated that she wouldn't be able to go farther than the sandy shore. She wasn't fearful, but she wouldn't be foolish enough to drag herself through an unknown forest where she could easily be caught. Knowing that she was the only dweller in her territory to sit on the shore of Kova would have to be fulfilling enough.

Her tail slapped the sea, and she was only a few paces from the sandy shore. The edge of the forest appeared no different than the one on the opposite side. But she couldn't see what lurked inside.

Tavarra let the waves push her forward, shoving her body the remainder of the way. Her palm touched the sand, and something moved. She stared down, watching the ripple unfold before her eyes. It wasn't the waves—it was the sand.

Pulling herself to a sitting position, Tavarra stayed near the water as the sand created small waves. The boats shifted back and forth, and she couldn't help but fall in love with what she was seeing.

Wicked? I think not.

As though answering her thoughts, voices cooed from behind her, "Sea dweller."

She whirled to the side. No one was there.

"Sea dweller." The words sounded again.

A rustling of wings came from the trees, and bright blue eyes sprinkled in its wake.

Her blood froze as the old ships creaked and sang their old forgotten songs. The waves of the sand grew more rapid, and if she didn't go back to the sea, she feared the grains would bury her alive. At that moment, Tavarra truly was afraid. She scampered to her stomach as the sand crashed against her tail. With a quick thrust, she rolled into the black murkiness, letting it sweep her away and refusing to glance back.

Something about those voices stayed with her as she flew through the liquid. Perhaps it had all been in her head. That was what she hoped, anyway.

She could have sworn something from that sand lingered with her as she swam past the mer who called to her once again, their cold fingertips brushing her skin, attempting to lure her into becoming one of their playthings.

The colors of her home materialized. She was safe, and she pretended as if going to Kova had never occurred. It was as if nothing had happened at all.

Tavarra woke to whisperings of something, but it was only from the memory she had tucked and buried away. Her younger self loved the adventure, the happiness, the free spirit of it all, but after visiting Kova for that short time, she hadn't needed to discover more about abandoned lands, whispering from trees, or blackened waters. She had turned her focus to the side of Laith, where humans thrived, where stories were told, dances took place, and people fell in love.

But as she grew to learn, that side of Laith wasn't perfect either. Nothing was.

"How do you feel about us gathering fish?" Vaden asked, stretching his muscular arms, then rubbing his eyes.

There were rations in her pack, but she wanted them to last. As a sea dweller, she was fast under the sea and could catch multiple fish. Even as a cursed creature she could, but as a human … she wasn't sure.

"I think I can hold onto the anchor and grab a few," she said, looking over the edge of the boat. "I know their movements. Do you know how to swim?"

"I do not, but I can try."

An image flashed through her head of him jumping in and just sinking straight to the bottom. "I think you better stay up here and keep watch, wouldn't want you drowning. How did you expect us to catch fish together then?"

"I did not think that far ahead."

Sighing, Tavarra shook her head. "I'm going to remove my clothing. You're not strange about that like the humans, are you?"

"My eyes will only ever be for one woman. I walk these lands in solitude until the day I die."

"That's not what I meant, but I got the answer I needed."

Tavarra kicked off her boots and tore off her tunic and trousers. She wanted to go right in, but she stopped for a moment, catching herself before diving straight into the water. Using legs wasn't as fast—she had discovered that in the lake with Eza, where she had to relearn how to swim by using new movements.

Either way, she would try. Tavarra dove down into the warm water, dropping farther into a sea of colored fish. She may be human, but they still flocked to her as if she wasn't, as though the color of her hair was a true beacon.

As the fish paraded around her, Tavarra reached and grasped one, then another. Quickly, she swam up and tossed them to Vaden, repeating her motions a few more times until they had enough to eat between the three of them.

Tavarra waded to the side of the ship and pulled herself up by the dangling rope. As soon as she barreled over to the floor of the deck, she exchanged glances with Vaden … and Perin.

"What are you doing?" Perin's expression looked lost while holding both hands up, as if he had never seen a naked woman before. Perhaps he hadn't.

"Collecting food for us to eat. Vaden doesn't know how to swim." Tavarra stood and walked to where the jovkin was using her daggers to cut into the fish.

"*Naked*?" Perin asked incredulously. He managed to keep his eyes on her face.

"I was naked when I was a sea dweller," Tavarra said, picking up her tunic and trousers. "And if you haven't noticed, Vaden is naked, too. So it looks as though you're the one left out." She took a step closer to him, a heat spreading within her. "However, I do remember seeing you very much naked, Perin."

Closing his eyes, he let out a breath. "You win. But next time, let me know, and I can help."

"What's the first thing you said?" She grinned.

"You won this"—he held up his hands a minuscule amount apart—"tiny battle."

Tavarra rolled her eyes and tugged her clothes on over her still-wet body, leaving her feet bare. "How are you feeling? Hungry?"

"I'm not really sure at the moment."

"I think you need to eat the fish." She paused, looking at his clammy forehead. "Raw, right? That's our only option, anyway."

"Yeah."

She tossed a few his way.

"Wait, we have no way to cook these?" Vaden asked.

"Would you want to set the boat on fire? I have dried meat in the pack and some fruit, if you prefer."

"I'll eat those later." Vaden covered his nostrils and bit into the fish's flesh that he had already stripped from the bone. Perin used his blade and stuffed bits into his mouth. As he ate, he didn't have the same expression as he had when eating the man on the pier. This looked to be more of a chore for him than enjoyment.

"What's wrong?" she asked.

"It tastes like dirt." Perin thrust the final piece in between his lips.

"If it comes down to it," Vaden said, "you can cut off my arm and eat it. I only need one."

"*What*?" Tavarra and Perin both said simultaneously, jerking their heads up.

"If it ever comes down to Tavarra and me, just take a piece from me."

"I'm fine," Perin replied, looking nothing like he was fine. "Let's not say things like that again. We'll get to Kova, I'll find this lavender liquid there, then we'll make way for the Stone." His head turned to Vaden. "You're not planning to go back to the village and try to live there, are you?"

"What's wrong if he did?" Tavarra piped in.

"I didn't say he couldn't. I just don't know if people would accept him there."

"No one questioned me or … Eza staying there." The memory didn't burn as much as she remembered how welcoming Lana was, she didn't ask questions about who they were or what they were—just accepted them. She knew Lana would accept Vaden, but she wasn't so sure if Rhona would. She could quite possibly have her brother's attitude.

"I do not want to live in any villages," Vaden said.

"There's your answer." Perin's lips twitched as he looked at Tavarra. "Now, we need to think about what we're going to do when we land in Kova."

Tavarra remembered the sound of those things hidden in the trees, calling to her. She wondered if she would hear them again.

Fifteen

Perin

Half the day had passed, and Tavarra had gone down below deck to get some rest. Perin stayed above because he felt it was still better to keep his distance from her—to keep her safe.

He lifted the liquid from the barrel to his lips and drank several handfuls of water. The taste of dirt from the raw fish was still there, or maybe it wasn't, but he could still imagine the flavor. Running his tongue along the roof of his mouth, he felt better. His stomach hadn't ruptured with aches, but he continued to be wary about everything.

"So, tell me about you," Vaden said, trying to start another conversation.

Perin just wanted to sit in silence. Rubbing his forehead in obvious irritation, he turned to the jovkin. "There's nothing to tell. But you might want to keep your distance, too, because, along the way, I've not only eaten a man but a jovkin as well."

"And so has Tavarra." Vaden made the comeback quickly.

Perin's lips parted, then closed at a loss for words because that was true.

"We are filled with tales, so many inside of us, waiting to be told," the jovkin continued.

Blowing out a breath, Perin sat with his back propped

against the wall of the boat. "Why don't you start with you, then. How did you become so ... you?"

Vaden plopped down right beside Perin, the jovkin's arm almost touching his. He hadn't listened very well.

"Tavarra hasn't heard this one, so it's kind of a gift to you."

Perin just arched a brow.

"I come from a long line of female jovkins who mated and raised their one offspring alone. Each female handed their tale down from a greater jovkin."

"Sounds prolific." Perin wasn't the least bit impressed by this. His villages passed down stories, too.

Vaden held up a hand, shushing him. "Junah was *very* prolific, from the tale anyway."

At the name, Perin's eyes expanded in size, and he couldn't remember how to blink for several long seconds.

"Junah?" he finally murmured. It couldn't be the same jovkin, could it? People had the same names all the time. But did jovkins?

"Yes, she had raised two bats and their—"

"Named Bray and Brenik," Perin straightened, cutting off the jovkin.

"Yes! How did you know?" For the first time, Vaden looked to be the one confused and Perin felt like he had the upper hand, if only for that moment.

"Because I know the story. My half-sister is from the same line as Bray." From the tale, Junah had been unlike others of the species, and Perin had never truly believed that she was any different from the jovkins he'd seen. But maybe she was.

"I don't understand. Brayora was a tiny bat." Vaden moved his hands and demonstrated the size, accurately.

Sighing, Perin told Vaden the story. Vaden knew already that the humans had crossed over because of Luca, but he hadn't known that he was Bray's son or that she could shift from bat to human.

"I must meet your sister one day."

"Possibly," Perin said. "But, you still need to finish the story about Junah."

Vaden scratched the side of his face. "After Brayora and Brenik left, Junah missed the company and decided to birth a child of her own. That jovkin had a child and that jovkin had a child and—"

"I get the point," Perin interrupted. "When Bray returned to Laith, she never found Junah again, though."

"She had been killed when her child was only seven full seasons old, and that jovkin chose not to be like the others of our kind."

Perin ran a hand over his jaw, thinking that something still didn't make any sense. "Yet she still mated?"

"Cannot deny the need for pleasures."

Warmth ran up Perin's throat and cheeks, causing them to redden. He wouldn't know—he'd never been with a woman. All he'd ever experienced was that one kiss with Tavarra and the thought alone was enough to set him on a different kind of fire because it was… It was … probably only the heat of the moment because of her sadness about Eza.

He couldn't help but think of Tavarra's body, her glorious body, the one he'd tried so damn hard earlier to keep his eyes off of. Yet he'd glimpsed it as she'd climbed up the side of the boat before spilling to the deck.

He'd had some sort of feelings stirring for her ever since she first had him by the throat. No one—no one—had ever gotten the best of him; had gotten him to the ground so quickly the way she had. Rhona had once, but he'd let her win. However, Tavarra had taken him by complete surprise. Even when he knew he was going to be stabbed by Rhona's mother, Perin had seen it coming and only had enough time to get his sister out of the way.

Things were much different now, though, and Tavarra should have stayed behind. Yet she was here now, and he'd have to not only keep her safe from whatever was on Kova but from himself as well.

The boat swayed, and Perin glanced up. A loud bang reverberated, making the boat rock harder.

Unsheathing his sword, Perin jumped to his feet and peered over the edge.

"What was that?" Vaden asked, appearing beside him.

Stomping feet clomped against the deck from behind them right as Tavarra came running up from below. "Damn it!" she shouted.

Another hard strike to the boat came again, and Perin had to grab hold of the edge to keep from falling. "What is it?"

She clasped her hands to her head and ground her teeth. "The mer, or what you would think of as mermaids."

"What are they doing?"

"Not trying to warn us what lies ahead or anything." She hurried and looked over the side. "They're most likely going to try to lure us down to their lair."

"To eat us?" Vaden asked.

"No, no," Tavarra answered. "They aren't that savage like Perin and I have been. They'll just let you die, dance with your corpse, watch it rot, then play with your bones."

Horrified, Vaden shouted down to the water. "Stop!"

Perin couldn't see anything except for the swishing of water. Tavarra stood frozen in place, staring straight ahead; at no one, at nothing, lost in her own head. He moved toward her, placing both of his hands on her cheeks. "What is it?"

"It's just, this reminds me of when I went to Kova's shore the one time," she whispered. "It wasn't the mer I feared then, or now, but what comes after. On the shore, the sand *moved*, and there was something there that called out to me."

"Do you need to go back to shore?" He would turn the boat around right that second if she said yes.

"No."

He dropped his hands from her cheeks, realizing just then what he was doing. "Okay, then. Just say the word if you need to.”

Tavarra shook her head, right as the pounding flared up again, the boat rocking even harder, and she continued to stand still. “I just don’t want to see any of them,” she whispered. “Even if they are only mer, they will still remind me of her.”

Her sister. Nezarra.

“You don’t have to.” Perin hurried to the other side where Vaden stood shouting over the edge at someone. His facial coloring was taking on a greenish hue, as if he was becoming nauseous.

Down below, Perin spotted something rising from beneath the surface. It was a female with long white hair, blackened teeth in the shape of thorns, onyx eyes, and a sunken pale-white face. She appeared skeletal as if there was no muscle beneath, only skin attached to bone. She looked nothing like the mermaids of the stories he’d heard.

“Join us,” the mermaid called up, running her arms across the top of the water as though that would entice him. “Or we will make you come below.”

“He’s not going anywhere!” Tavarra growled down, more enraged than he’d ever seen. She managed to snap out of wherever her emotions had taken her.

Another head protruded from the water. A merman with hair just as white as the female, his shoulders were broad but still skeletal. If there had been muscle beneath, then his chest would have been as strong as iron. The merman slapped the boat, making it tip to the side and almost fall over—the male still had strength in those bones. Perin grasped the wooden rail and placed his boot against the wall to keep himself steady.

“Come on,” the male cooed, almost seductively. “You can have your own throne if you join us.”

“Fuck off,” Perin shouted.

“I think it’s only those two,” Tavarra said, scanning the water with a dagger in hand.

“I remember you.” The mermaid pointed a frail finger at

Tavarra. "You could have stayed to become a queen, but instead, you left."

"Queen of the corpses?" Tavarra seethed.

"Now you will become one of the corpses," the merman sang, striking the side of the ship. "And your bones will be ours to do with as we please."

Perin dropped his sword and retrieved his dagger, having had enough of this shit. "You're sure it's just the two?" He didn't want to draw the notice of a whole clan that could easily knock the ship over.

"Only one way to find out," Tavarra said, right as she let her dagger fly, hitting the female's forehead.

The merman whirled around to look at the female, his lips pursing with anger. "What have you done?"

As the male turned back to the boat, Perin threw his dagger. It landed right in the left eye. A huff of air left the merman's lips as scarlet dripped from the blow.

They paused and stared out at the two floating mer.

"We can't leave the bodies there," Tavarra rushed the words out.

"Why not?"

"Because if the other mer find them, then our crossing to Kova, or back from there, won't have a very pleasant outcome. We can dump the bodies when we get farther away from their territory."

"How do you want us to get the bodies up here?" Vaden asked, already moving toward the rope.

"I'll go in and get them. You two pull," Perin said, tearing his shirt over his head, tugging off his boots, then diving into the sea. The warm water thrust against his strong body as he stroked his way to the first floating female. He hurriedly wrapped the rope around her thin form, and Tavarra and Vaden hauled her up. After Tavarra tossed the rope back down, he repeated his previous movements with the male.

As Tavarra lifted the merman, Perin climbed his way back

up and met her gaze. "You did that by yourself?" he asked.

"I told Vaden to let me see if I could. Something feels off at times, as though I'm stronger on occasion. It's very strange."

The same type of abilities, like the ones humans were gifted when they first crossed over from Earth. They had been dying out since humans had started to adjust to the land, but the Stone must have known that Tavarra would need hers. "I think you may be uncovering your ability, just as Rhona and Quil had done."

"Let me see." She bent over and tried to pick up the body. Her face took on a red hue as she lifted him a fraction from the floor and dropped him. "I don't know if that's it."

He turned to Vaden, who was staring at Perin's crisscrossing scars that coated his entire chest and back. The jovkin didn't ask any questions, and Tavarra had already seen them all before, but it didn't make him feel any less ashamed.

Before her, no one else had seen them besides his father, or Lana's few moments while tending to his leg wound. At night, Perin would bathe alone when it was dark, and no one could see what was there.

Out of nowhere, an ache shot through Perin's stomach, and he dropped to one knee.

Tavarra bent down beside him. "You need to eat, don't you?" Her attention turned to the dead guests. "You're just in luck since we have two fresh carcasses."

Perin looked over at the ghastly creatures with barely any muscle. "I'm not eating them." What he wanted to say was that he didn't want to monstrously eat anything else in front of her.

"Think about all the things they have possibly done to other humans or to creatures below the sea. You don't have to feel bad about this one, all right?"

Perin stroked a hand down his face, peering at the two bodies as his stomach thumped over and over. He had to do it because, if not, the only other two options were Tavarra or

Vaden, and he would slit his own throat before letting that happen.

"Which one?" she asked, retrieving her dagger from the female's forehead, then ticking it back and forth between the bodies.

"I guess the male. He seemed more of an ass."

"A jest?" Tavarra laughed softly, the sound beautiful. She brought up her dagger and sunk it into the merman's chest, slicing it down just past his navel. "Dig in."

"If it will make you feel more comfortable, we'll go below deck." She turned around and walked away, but Vaden stayed by his side.

"Would you feel better if I joined in, so you aren't the only one?" Vaden asked, appearing even more nauseous because he didn't want to actually eat the raw meat.

"Just go, Vaden." Perin sighed.

Now alone, Perin focused on the incision Tavarra had made. The fresh meat from inside the open wound wafted straight into Perin's nostrils, and the pain within his stomach turned into a ravenous roar. Closing his eyes, he pretended it was cooked rabbit meat that he was placing against his tongue. Each bite felt better than the last.

When he finished, Perin filled a bucket with salt water and cleaned his face and hands, removing any sign of blood. He had to remember that these two were horrible creatures, but the man he'd killed before, he had known nothing about him. Humans could be many types of things.

Quietly, he slid his shirt back on and called down to Tavarra, "Can I speak to you for a moment?"

She didn't call back, but he could hear the sound of her feet against the wood. Her eyebrows furrowed as she climbed out. "What's wrong?"

"I was just thinking…" He stared at the charcoal-gray clouds in the sky.

"This 'thinking' doesn't seem good," she said. "These

thoughts sound as though they are conflicting, a war with one's self."

"We're going through ridiculous lengths here just to make it so my stomach doesn't hurt. When I discussed this quest with the Stone, I didn't think much of it. I thought I would just hop on a boat, sail across the sea, come back, and find Rhona. But this is such a fucking mess. I just filleted this merman."

"Actually, I filleted him first," Tavarra said. "But do go on."

Thoughts swirled in Perin's head—of his father, of himself, of what could have been, of what now could be. "I think we should turn around and end this."

"You want to hold onto this curse? Because I did that for seven years, and I can tell you right now that it isn't a life," she spat.

"That's the difference, you didn't know what you were doing!" Perin pointed to the dead body of the merman. "You see him? I *remember* eating a few of his organs. I'm not sure which ones, but I remember it clear as day."

"I understand that but—"

"Turn the boat around, and you can end me now." Perin's words came out in a choked cry, and he hated himself for it. "I should have stayed below the ground."

"You want me to *murder* you? Do you have any idea what your sister would do if she found out? You know, if Rhona was here, she would have thrown daggers at those mer herself, then made you eat them, too."

"I can't eat anyone else that is human or resembles one. I *can't.*"

"Then we'll have to find whatever creatures are on Kova, but please survive!" she practically pleaded.

His chest tightened at that, but he bit the middle of his lip and shook his head. Perin had always felt like a failure in his life—to himself, to his sister—and this was almost deranged.

"You know what Eza would say if she were here," Tavarra

spoke without tears, and he waited for her to continue. "She would say, 'We all have to do what we have to do to survive. And you're going to survive.'"

A tear slipped from his eye, and he wiped it away. "I need help." He struggled to admit that aloud.

"You helped me, and I'm going to help you," she promised.

Tavarra grabbed his hand and gave it a gentle squeeze. The sound of Vaden climbing up from below deck made Perin scoot back.

"I'm going to go lay down for a little while." He needed to be alone, wanted to be alone, wanted to be back underground, even if he was still awake down there.

You're such a failure, always the failure. You're nothing, but underneath it all, you know you're just like me. His father's words pounded over and over in his head.

Once below deck, Perin curled onto his side and hugged his knees to his chest and cried, let out years and years of tears that he'd held back. Down here, he felt safe. Down here, he felt as if the darkness could sweep him away. He always pushed everything aside that he had to in order to feel okay, but nothing was okay, and even if he got this lavender liquid to the Stone, what if it decided not to change him back anyway?

Sixteen

Tavarra

The night had already fallen, and Perin hadn't come back up to the deck. Tavarra tossed and turned in the darkness.

"You should go and check on him," Vaden suggested, noticing her inability to sleep.

"I think he wants to be alone." *But did he ever leave you alone when you wanted to be?* He had not—he had chosen to watch over her.

"I've got it all handled." Vaden pointed at the helm. "If the boat turns, I know how to use the wheel."

"Fine, you're becoming quite the captain. But shout if you need me." From her pack, Tavarra pulled out a glass mixture of fairy wings and fireflies. She shook it, and a soft blue lit up the deck of the boat. Holding out the light, she stepped down the ladder. Perin lay on his side, his lips slightly parted, breathing deeply.

Quietly, she sat across from his sleeping form to watch over him. Her eyes started to get heavy, and she decided to close them for only a moment.

"Why are you down here?" Perin whispered.

Fully awake, Tavarra straightened and set the blue light in between them. "I didn't realize this was your room only."

"It's not," he said, almost coldly. "I can go up there, and you can stay down here."

"No. I have a better idea. You go back to sleep," she replied.

He pulled himself up to a sitting position and rested his face in his hands. "I'm sorry, I shouldn't have snapped like that. I don't think I can go back to sleep, either."

"We can talk if you want?"

"Should I call you Queen Tavarra now? You never told me about the merpeople offering you a royal spot in their clan." He smirked, and she caught a glimpse of the old Perin. The one she had spent time with for several days, who wasn't only stubborn but also loyal and kind.

"Yeah, a queen of the corpses." Her insides shivered at the thought of being surrounded by decaying bodies and the mer playing with them.

"I still like the ring of Queen Tavarra."

"It does sound fascinating, doesn't it?"

Perin let out a small chuckle, then covered his mouth to yawn. In the soft blue light, his eyes appeared tired with bags beneath them. He looked pitiful, really. So she reached out a hand and ran it gently through his hair. He flinched for a moment—a habit courtesy of his father—before relaxing and shutting his eyes.

"Get some rest," she said.

"What if something happens?" He was worrying way more than she ever did in her seven years as the beast.

"I've got a dagger right here, and a jovkin above." She pulled the weapon from her waist and stabbed it into the wood. "I think we can handle you."

"So confident." He rolled his eyes, but his lips twitched at the same time.

Tavarra wanted to let him get some sleep without her hovering, but a part of her was afraid that if she left, he would disappear again. She didn't want to use the word die, but even while coming down here, she secretly feared that she would find a dead body because that's what things did around her—they *died*.

During his sleep, Perin didn't move, didn't shake with nightmares, but that didn't mean he didn't have them. Even in this state, where he should be relaxing, he still had the line between his two eyebrows and the corners of his lips pulled down.

As she continued to curiously wonder what went on while he was sleeping, she managed to find some rest of her own. Her old dweller self would have wanted to curl up beside him and listen to the *tick, tick, ticks* of his heartbeat. The second side of her cared more about him being all right, and the third part of her—the one she had hidden away—was worried about the shore of Kova.

Tavarra's eyes flicked open to the morning's light, and Perin was no longer in the room. There was a blanket wrapped around her and she relaxed into the fabric. The day before slid into her mind—she hurried and threw the blanket off, quickly sitting up. He had thought about dying. What if? What if? She flew up the steps. What if he had jumped off the ship? Or worse?

Her heart sat frozen in her chest until she spotted him on the other side of the boat beside Vaden. For some reason, the jovkin had her sword in his hands. Perin swung, knocking the weapon from Vaden's grasp.

"No!" Tavarra shouted. "Stop! Don't hurt him."

They both turned to her, cocking their heads.

"Perin is only teaching me how to use a sword," Vaden said, scooping the blade back up.

"It looked as though he was teaching you how to have it knocked out of your hands!" she seethed.

"This is the twentieth time I've tried, and the same thing happens again and again."

"Twentieth?" Tavarra wanted to tell Vaden that maybe jovkins weren't meant to know how to fight with swords.

"Perhaps this isn't my day." Vaden shrugged.

Tavarra took the sword from Vaden's hand and looked toward Perin. "Show me."

The side of Perin's lips quirked. "It will take longer than this boat ride to learn."

Eza could talk Tavarra into learning almost anything, but the bat had never known the art of swords. It was a strange dance that Tavarra didn't know if she could ever perfect, but she had spied on humans so many times with Eza that she knew some things.

"We'll see about that, won't we?"

"I won't go easy on you," he said, bringing the sword up, then swiping it to the right and releasing a *whoosh* as the blade kissed the wind.

"I don't want easy." Then she hurled herself at him, holding her weapon out in front of her. Automatically, Perin's sword went up and cracked against hers in an almost delicate rumble that vibrated throughout her arm. He pushed her back—she kept her balance.

"I thought you didn't know how to use a sword?" Perin asked as he swung his weapon, striking hers back and forth.

"I don't, but I've watched long enough to see how the game is played."

"Game, huh?" He chuckled, his frown, his expression, all of it free in that moment and making him look young, so very young.

Tavarra went right and dodged back. He tapped her blade and whirled away, coming up again, until his blade caught hers. Each pressed and pressed—her strength matching his undeniable one, maybe hers was even stronger. But how was that possible? Then an ache formed in her wrist and she had to give, but she didn't drop the sword as she stepped back.

A slow clap echoed in the corner, coming from Vaden, but she didn't avert her eyes. She knew if she got distracted that Perin wouldn't stop just because she glanced away.

It helped that she and Perin were the same size. If Tavarra had been smaller, she would have been on the ground already, unless she was Rhona.

She swung her sword, and it pressed against his like before, and she pushed harder this time, her eyes finding his bright blue ones. She stared at him and he watched her. Never once did she forget about her sword being on his, but something in his gaze changed and he released his blade from hers. "That was good, you're a natural."

Tavarra didn't understand what was wrong, what had just happened with his change in mood. It made her blood boil. She didn't know what she did to make his smile vanish. With a thrust, she slammed the sword into the wood and turned to walk away.

Perin grabbed her by the shoulder.

"What?" she asked, voice hard.

"I just..." His eyes searched hers, and she didn't know what he was looking for.

"Yes?"

Before he could answer, Vaden shouted, "Tavarra!"

She turned to the direction of the jovkin's voice. Up ahead, the waves of the sea were swelling, growing in size. The boat rocked and creaked as a wave splashed against it, knocking Tavarra to her backside. A hand clasped hers, and Perin yanked her up.

"The sea doesn't want us to go," she whispered, rubbing the sore spot from her fall.

"Well, that's too damn bad." Perin stared ahead.

"The sea will have to let us," she said. "It's just a warning."

They weren't that far from shore, and they needed to get rid of the mer. "Let's drop the mer here. No one from under comes this way." Except for her—the one time, so very long ago.

Vaden lifted the female and shoved her overboard, a splash sounding, and bubbles rising. Another wave struck the boat as Tavarra and Perin threw the male in next.

"I have a feeling once we get past the shore, things will be difficult." Tavarra shook out her hands. "Are you up for the challenge?"

"I live for the challenge." Perin lifted a handful of water to his mouth.

"You're going to have to think of your hunger as a challenge. One you want to control. Can you do that?" Her beast was never able to do that, but maybe his could be tamed.

His eyes softened for a moment as he looked at her, then his frown was back. "I don't know."

Vaden took hold of the helm as the waves grew fiercer. Tavarra and Perin grasped onto the rail. The jovkin kept the boat from turning as it went through massive swells, large amounts of water splashing her.

Tavarra pressed her hand to cover her mouth, her stomach tossing back and forth. She leaned over the edge, gripping the rail, and expelling the entirety of her last meal. Right when she went to pull herself up, she heaved again, but nothing came out that time. The up and down motions were making her dizzier and dizzier.

"Are you all right?" Perin asked.

"No!" she shouted over the loud noise. "But whatever you do, keep your food down. I don't care if you have to swallow your bile."

"I don't even feel sick!" he shouted back.

"Lucky you!" Still holding firmly onto the rail, she thought of something. Not only had she felt trapped beneath the ocean, but now she felt the same above it as well. Once she got back to shore, she would only ever stare out at the sea from a distance, she would never sail or swim in it again.

The sky faded to a blood-red as the two suns became hidden by darkening clouds. Suddenly, cool sprinkles fell to her skin, as though their day couldn't get any worse.

"Shit," Perin said.

"Shit is right," she agreed.

"Get down below," Vaden yelled. "I'll steer."

"A little rain never hurt anyone." She was used to getting drenched all the time when she lived outdoors with Eza. She slept in it, ran through it, ate in it, sulked in it. But right now, she would do anything to get away from looking at the ocean and any water.

She took Vaden's offer and went below deck. Tavarra dropped to her knees and leaned her back against the wall.

A few moments later, Perin came down to check on her.

"I need to get off this boat," she said, her stomach churning again. "I *need* to get off this boat."

Perin sat down beside her and struck his head against the wall. "This is all because you didn't listen to me."

"What?" She leaned forward and arched a brow.

"I told you to stay back on shore," he said, matter of fact.

Tavarra was a hair's breadth from Perin. "If you say that one more time, so help me. I'll—"

"You'll what?" Perin interrupted. "Kill me?"

Tavarra pulled back as if he had struck her with his blade. "That's not funny. You already know I thought you actually died."

"You still have the ring." His eyes fell to the necklace around her throat, the one she didn't ever remove, except for when that bastard Ian took it.

"Of course I do, you fool! What did you think I was going to do with it? Toss it away?"

"You could have left it with me?" His tone didn't sound as if he had wanted it buried with him. It was more of a question.

"Do you want it back?"

She reached for the ring, and he stopped her, his gaze locking on hers, an emotion brewing there. "Never."

With a nod, she broke their stare and tucked the objects inside her shirt. "Good. It's mine."

When he didn't say anything, she let out a sigh and turned to him once more. She placed her hands on his cheeks, wanting to press her forehead to his. "What I need you to do for me once we get to Kova is to be brave and not act a fool. If we're going to do this together, it's because we both want to. Can you do this?"

He closed his eyes and leaned forward until she thought his lips would brush hers ever so softly. "My father's dead."

Tavarra's expression became confused, and her stomach dropped. "Yes, Perin, he's gone." Was he starting to lose his memories with this forsaken curse?

"I keep having these dreams that he isn't." He paused. "Or nightmares, really, about him waking up the way I did. I know he wasn't buried where I was, but what if?"

Something in Tavarra stiffened, her heart constricting. She assumed that once Perin's father died that he would be okay, but he still wasn't. At least, not completely. "He won't."

"I beheaded him just in case," he whispered, almost ashamed.

"We should have done that."

Perin was a good man even though he irritated her sometimes to no end, but most of all Tavarra wanted to help him as he had with her that night in the forest after Eza. She pressed her forehead to his, the way she had the night they kissed. "Believe in yourself." She wanted to shake him, but at the same time, she wanted to lean forward and kiss him.

Pushing himself from her, Perin looked away. "I can't do this right now."

"Why?" Tavarra wanted to scream in his face.

"Because you smell too damn good." He appeared as though he'd had too much wine to drink.

Her eyes widened, and she scooted back enough for him to relax. "You don't have—"

Something collided with the boat, causing it to jolt. She and Perin exchanged a glance before they darted up the steps to Vaden.

"What's going on?" Perin asked.

"Looks like we struck sand." Vaden pointed up ahead.

As she followed the direction of his finger, sure enough, she was back—same as when she had been twelve years old. Except this time, she could see everything more clearly. Perin scanned the area with an unreadable expression.

The trunks of the trees were dark green with sapphire-colored leaves. Birds, or something, squawked in the distance. That, at least, meant there were signs of some sort of life. There were no whispers in the trees or the sand swelling to create waves.

"Where do we go now?" Vaden asked.

"The Stone said to head south and pass through bramble with silver thorns," Perin said. "Apparently, we'll know when we see this lake of lavender miracles."

Leaping from the boat after gathering her things, Tavarra's boots crushed the sand, and a blast of wind struck her. "Welcome home," it seemed to say.

Seventeen

Tavarra

Tavarra's feet struck the sand, and she expected it to move.

It didn't—it remained perfectly still. Perin and Vaden both hopped down beside her with suspicion.

Perin adjusted his pack as Tavarra eyed the forest with diligence, taking careful steps forward. She cocked her head and listened for any other sounds besides the cawing creatures that she couldn't see. The closer Tavarra got, the more she could see—like the vines snaking their way up the bellies of the trees. On the blue leaves, the veins appeared to be more of a black.

"The Stone told you to head south," Tavarra said. "We shouldn't procrastinate. Let's go."

Perin's hand lightly brushed over his stomach before he retrieved his sword. "Agreed."

Was he hungry now? He had mentioned the way she smelled, but he hadn't tried to attack her. Yet.

Vaden stood in a stance, almost primal. She hadn't truly seen him like this, as though he were ready to fight if trouble started.

They inched closer to the trees. Tavarra stared up into the branches where the squawking came from. High up, she noticed that the creatures were midnight-blue birds. She had to squint her eyes to make sure she wasn't seeing double because each bird had not one head but two. On both their heads sat long, curving beaks that ended in a sharp point.

As she stepped forward through the trees, a bird landed on Perin's shoulder and squawked in his ear. He shoved it off.

"I don't know if you should have done that…" Vaden whispered.

"You're right," Tavarra said. "He should have decapitated it, then tried to eat it."

Shaking his head, Perin walked ahead. Tavarra followed, finding the ground firm and covered in thick swirling grass and weeds blooming black flowers with white centers. A gust of wind shot past them, rifling her hair.

From the birds, the squawking turned into a loud ticking sound growing in frequency. In a cloud of uproarious thunder, the birds swarmed down. Perin swung his sword, Tavarra withdrew hers, and Vaden swatted at them with his hands.

Something snatched Perin's foot and tossed him backward. He rolled around, finding a vine latched around his foot. Tavarra lifted her sword and hurried after him. Two vines shot forward, binding her wrists. She let out an angry shout, not being able to spot Vaden. Perin managed to swing his sword, releasing the hold of the vine.

Tavarra kicked her leg up, trying to snap the plant in half. Perin ran forward and brought his blade down, but before it landed its blow, two more vines snatched his wrists.

"What the fuck is going on?" he bellowed.

"I don't know!" Focusing as hard as she could, she gave a hard yank with her right wrist, breaking the vine. With her sword, Tavarra sliced the other one and moved for Perin.

"Where's Vaden?" she asked him as she broke his vines in half, setting him free. Letting out a frustrated sigh, she searched around. The jovkin was nowhere.

"Up there!" Perin's voice was low over all the uproar

coming from the birds. They had him in the air.

As the birds spread apart, it wasn't them that held Vaden hostage, but branches confining him and covering his mouth.

A creak, then a groan came as a long, gnarled limb shot upward, wrapping around Vaden's middle. Tavarra was pulled from her staring spell when another branch grasped her hand holding the sword. Several curses escaped her mouth as she struggled to get herself out.

In the middle of the trunk standing across from her, the bark spread apart, opening up to its … mouth? The birds swarmed around Vaden's body as the limb dragged him inside the open space. Perin tried to get through the cacophony of birds, but he couldn't. The winged creatures prevented Vaden's escape, and the tree closed up with a groan.

Tavarra's heart kicked up notch after notch, remembering the stories of humans going missing in Kova. She didn't know what had happened to the lost humans, but now she knew the fate of at least some of them.

Perin yelled at Tavarra as a branch folded around his waist. "Find your strength, Tavarra!"

"I don't know if I can!" She had felt it several times lately, and it was at its strongest when she had been dueling with Perin. Closing her eyes, she tried to tap into whatever she could and gave a hard yank, ripping away from the limb. The tree cried in pain with an agonizing squeal as the branch pulled back.

With the dagger at her waist, she hurled herself forward and stabbed the branch holding onto Perin, hacking at it until it finally gave way with the same high-pitched squeals.

Tavarra and Perin sprinted for the tree where Vaden was trapped. Perin ran his palm against the bark, trying to find the seal. She couldn't see one, so she took her dagger and thrust it forward. Her weapon didn't even penetrate. Stepping to the side, she watched as Perin swung his sword, leaving no sign of a single notch.

Around them, the world had quieted except for the two-headed birds sprinkled across the branches of the tree where Vaden was, only lightly squawking now.

"Vaden!" Tavarra pounded on the trunk, screaming, wishing her strength was strong enough to uproot trees. But she had never been able to do that.

She expected no answer because he was probably already dead, but then she heard his muffled voice, surprising her. "I'm in here."

"I don't know how to get you out!" Tavarra turned to Perin. "What should we do?

"Just go!" Vaden said.

"We're not leaving you in there," Perin said through gritted teeth, attempting to saw at the trunk with the tip of his sword.

"Three days," a voice called from somewhere in the tree.

Tavarra and Perin both glanced up to find only the two-headed creatures. Were the birds *talking* to them?

"The tree won't devour him for three days' time," the voice—female—said.

"I don't see anything." Perin furrowed his brow and backed up to get a better look.

"Is the tree talking? But the voice would have said 'I,' right?"

"No, it wasn't the tree," the female's voice came again. "It was me." Out from behind the trunk, a creature pushed one of the sapphire-leaved bushes out of the way. Her skin was so blue that it was almost black. The beastly creature reached just above Tavarra's waist with a silver eye and the other missing, along with pointed ears, a sharp nose, a protruding belly, and wrinkled skin. Tangled and ragged dark hair fell to the female's waist.

"Goblin?" Tavarra's lips parted. It looked like the descriptions from a story Brice had once told her of.

"What's it to you?" the creature snapped.

"Why are you on this side of Laith?"

"We quite like it here."

The goblin liked encountering trees that ate things?

"I know how to get the trees to open." She fully emerged from behind the bushes. "You're going to have to owe me something, though."

Perin shook his head because he was smart, and so was Tavarra, and both knew that bartering without knowing what was to be traded was most likely the wrong choice.

Sighing, Tavarra pursed her lips and asked, "What is it?"

"You three will join my clan at our feast."

Tavarra thought about the mer with their sharp teeth and their *lovely* feasts. Two of them they had killed. If something went wrong at this feast, with her strength hopefully back for good, she could easily swipe these beastly creatures and bring them a swift death.

There really wasn't much of a choice, and if they were able to get Vaden out, she could always choose to do whatever she wanted. Perin hadn't eaten, and maybe at this feast, they could get him something to hold back his appetite. Tavarra gripped the dagger tightly in her fist. "Fine, we'll join you for the feast."

The goblin brought her fist up and knocked on the trunk twice, then another two times, and finally blew against the bark with glittering white breath. The trunk split open, and a swaying Vaden spilled out, falling to his knees, his eyes connecting with the goblin's.

The goblin grinned, showing off teeth filled with holes and rot. "Join us for the feast." She flung herself forward and waved them to follow before disappearing behind the trunk.

"I hope you really don't trust that thing," Perin said, his eyes shifting around.

"Of course not." Tavarra followed his gaze and noticed not only had one tree been opened, but all of the trunks had. Buried inside most of them was at least one yellowing skeleton. Either they had been there long enough to rot, or the trees had sucked the life from their bones after the "three days." As if the trunks knew they were watching, each tree shifted and groaned as one by one, they resealed themselves.

"Let's hurry." Perin tilted his head to the south. "Watch your hands and feet for branches and vines."

There was no time to waste with trees that could capture them. They headed in the direction the goblin had vanished off in but found no sign of her. Along their path, they trekked past more black flowers that swayed in their direction. Tavarra could have sworn that each one was *smelling* them.

The forest wasn't large at all, and it connected to a wide rocky area with rows and rows of what looked like caves. A wall of flames stood high in front of the caves, burning brightly. Goblins of all shapes and sizes stood around the fire as it flickered and roared. More movement came from inside the caves where hundreds of tiny creatures hobbled out with weapons that looked like spears.

"It's safe to say let's skip the feast and find another way to continue south," Perin said.

"Yes, please," Vaden agreed.

Despite the obstacle ahead, Tavarra angled her gaze to the side to see how they could slip around them. Something smacked Tavarra's arm with a hard whack. "Ow." Before she could see what had hit her, a rain of blows thumped against her, Vaden, and Perin. Pebbles.

"Stop!" Vaden roared. They didn't stop. A large one pelted Vaden in the head, and he collapsed to his knees, eyes shut.

"Vaden!" she screamed. A hard strike landed on her ankle as goblins darted out from behind trees. She sliced her sword against several, splitting some into two and wounding others. Perin did the same.

From up in the trees, a net cascaded down on top of Tavarra and Perin before they could dodge out of the way. She tried to move her arms, but was confined to where she couldn't tear apart the material or use her sword. Her back was planted against Perin's, and the net tightened even more.

"Can you use your blade?" Perin asked, sounding annoyed.

"No, I can't even move!"

Goblins surrounded them. They were no longer throwing pebbles at them, but poking at them with sticks instead.

A tiny one hobbled onto the side of Tavarra's head, its weight heavy.

Another leaned over her—Tavarra recognized the missing eye. "You promised to come to the feast," the goblin said. "We haven't had a feast with new human meat in a while."

Tavarra had to think of what to do. They couldn't beg for their lives because the creatures wouldn't care. Tavarra wouldn't do that anyway. The goblin seemed to like bargaining, so maybe she could do that.

"How about a new trade?" Tavarra asked.

"Nothing can beat a feast." The goblin jabbed at Tavarra's forehead.

"We were sent here by the Stone of Desire to retrieve a lavender liquid. What if we were to gather some for you?"

The goblin stopped prodding at her. "Why would I require such nonsense? Besides, no one has made it past the swamp. Better you have a use for us here."

"We can," Perin said. "And do you know what you could do with this lavender liquid if you had it? The magic of it can help you go across this swamp yourselves, then you could use it on whatever you wanted to make an even better feast."

He was lying his ass off, and Tavarra tried not to roll her eyes. There was no way the goblin would believe that.

"And what if you two die and don't come back at all?" the goblin asked.

"Then I shall become your feast," Vaden answered. Tavarra thought that he had been knocked out, but he must have woken not too long after.

The goblin tapped at her chin while the other creatures

watched for their leader to answer. "It's a deal."

Tavarra couldn't believe it, or that Vaden was also putting his life at risk. They had to make it back because he couldn't be eaten—the way Eza had been… That time, Tavarra and Eza had made a trade between Rhona, Quil, and Perin that resulted in her friend's death. This time, she would make sure that didn't happen.

"A fair warning for if you make it across the hags' swamp, there are athers on the other side, ones we've been longing to make a meal of."

"Athers?" Perin asked, not having heard of the species before, either.

"Ones who will rip you to shreds and lap up your blood, quicker than we will." The goblin peered down at Tavarra. "And they won't be willing to do barters as we have."

"Remove the net," Perin urged, and she could hear the frustration laced behind it. Something was wrong. "Please."

"I suppose, but if you make a single move and try to back out, there will be consequences," she warned.

The net unraveled and was pulled away from them. Tavarra sat up, running a hand over her forehead and hair. "What do we call you by?"

"Lo," she said. "I do not care to know any of yours."

Tavarra could stab the goblin with her sword, but there wasn't any way she could defeat hundreds. Perin stayed quiet, and she glanced his way. His skin was starting to look a little pale, along with perspiration dotting across his brow and forehead. The suns in the sky were already fading for the night.

"Best you leave in the morning," Lo grumbled and focused her attention on Vaden. "You three can still join us for the feast, but the sacrifice will remain in the cave tied with us. *Safely* for the time being."

She hated the thought of Vaden being tied and left with these goblins, but it would have to do for now.

"You will enjoy this meal," Lo said.

She needed to get Perin something to eat, but would they even have anything bloody? Tavarra gave Perin a questioning glance, but he seemed to know what was happening.

Behind them, goblins were carrying the dead bodies that Perin and Tavarra had slaughtered. Her eyes widened as she looked between Perin and Vaden. Perin nodded and Vaden wrinkled his forehead. The goblins were going to eat their own kind? Willingly and without a curse?

Lo waved them on as the goblins poked sticks at Vaden, his hands tied behind his back. They followed Lo down a rocky slope until they reached the bottom covered in pebbles. In front of the fire, Lo raised a dagger and darted toward Tavarra. But she stopped and brought her blade across the throats of several goblins guarding Tavarra. "Now we have enough for a true feast," Lo roared and held her fists to the sky.

Four of the larger goblins lifted the dead bodies and carried them to the flames to be cooked.

"Lo," Tavarra rasped. "Could we have one uncooked?"

With a grin on her face, the goblin turned around. "I like you three, but I liked them, too. Death is always an option for those I like."

It wasn't an answer, but one of the goblins dropped a body at Tavarra's feet with a thump. She pushed Perin forward. He didn't move to pick up the food, nor turn to her. She grabbed his shoulder to look at his face and found his eyes clamped shut, his jaw clenched. With rough force, she shook him. His eyes flicked open, and he snapped his teeth at her. She jumped back and gasped. As recognition dawned on him, his glassy gaze cleared.

"I'm sorry." He held his hands up, horrified.

"Eat. All of it," Tavarra demanded, pointing at the body. It was of a good size, enough to fill them both, so it should be enough to hopefully last him until the next day.

With a nod, Perin lifted the goblin and brought it to his mouth, biting into a spot between the shoulder and head. As he chewed and blood gathered on his lips, Perin didn't look the least bit sickened anymore—it was as though it was the most wonderful thing he had ever tasted. That expression was nothing like Perin, and she knew it was something else building within him, making him feel this way, tearing him apart from the inside out. She would continue to help him fight it.

After a while, Lo and two other goblins brought back a cooked body for Vaden. "This is to keep you plump and fatten you up even more."

"Can you untie him?" Tavarra asked.

"No!" Lo shouted.

"Then, I'll feed him." Taking the cooked meat, Tavarra placed pieces into Vaden's mouth and took small portions for herself. The taste was bitter and too salty, but it would keep her strength up. She pulled the water from her pack and shared some with Vaden while Perin drank from his.

The goblins danced circles around the fire for what seemed like forever until it finally died down. Lo had left them alone, yet couldn't help but make another appearance. "We must take the sacrifice back to the cave now. If you are not back in three days, we eat him."

Three days? Was that enough time? She had no idea how long it would take for them to get the lavender liquid and bring it back.

"That is fine," Vaden answered for them, nodding in a way that showed it would be okay if they didn't return in time.

"Vaden—"

Lo hooted and roared a sound that vibrated the goblin's entire chest. A swarm of goblins, both small and large, prodded Vaden with their sticks and led him away while another cluster of the clan with spears gathered in front of Tavarra and Perin. Tavarra shouted to the jovkin to stay safe, but Perin seemed as if he was trying to hold back swinging his blade at the goblins.

"Try anything," Lo said, "you die." Then she turned and hobbled back to the cave.

Perin remained quiet as he rested on the rocky ground with his hands propped on his knees. Tavarra sat across from him while keeping her eyes on the line of goblins watching them from afar.

"You can bind me if you want." Perin lifted his head, voice soft. "I understand."

He had snapped at her, and that had caught her off guard. But as the beast, she had done much worse to him. "No, you're not at the point where we need to chain you. I know you're used to hiding your pain and not telling anyone about it. Your father is gone. Rhona is safe. I'm here, and you can tell me. What was going on earlier? What does it feel like?"

Letting out a heavy breath, Perin reclined his head back and gazed up at the sky. "The lower left side of my stomach was aching. It's been getting like that before I even feel any hunger. It seems to know that it needs to be fed before things can get worse."

For a moment, Tavarra formulated a plan to leave him behind when he fell asleep while she went and retrieved the liquid. The same way Rhona had left Quil behind to protect him. But that hadn't been Quil's journey, that was Rhona's. And this wasn't hers, it was Perin's.

In the end, she chose to stay. "I'll keep you fed while we're here, I promise."

Eighteen

Perin

Perin's eyes flicked open, his body in a world of pain. His muscles heavy, nerves inflamed, and his bones felt as if he had none at all, just a sea of liquid fire pooling inside him. All the pain struck right at his stomach, and he tried desperately to hold back a growl, his energy completely spent. His breathing came out in deep, endless heaves. Counting—one, two, three. One, two, three, four. One, two, three, four, *five*.

Bringing himself forward, Perin ran his hands through his hair, the pain slowly slipping away. It was as though his movements helped his body relax a bit. The morning had started to come, so he could already see Tavarra's outline, and hear her soft breathing.

As he stared at her gentle sleeping face, he wanted to brush his finger across her cheek, run it against a lock of her orange hair. But if he looked too long, he feared he'd want to press his teeth against her flesh.

Perin stood and stumbled forward, lifting his canteen to his lips to fill his thirst. The full dawn was about to break through the sky as he relieved himself behind a tree. A rustling of pebbles came from up ahead. The wind drifted by, rumpling his hair, and from the forest behind him, he could have sworn he heard whispers of the word, "human."

The pebbles rustled again, and he stepped out from behind the tree to go back and find Tavarra when Lo appeared. "Where do you think you're going? Trying to break our bargain?" she growled.

"No, I had to piss, is that a problem?" He looked behind him to the entrance of the forest. "I could have sworn I heard something back there."

"It's just the birds and the trees trying to lure you back inside. Like us, they are hungry." Lo's sharp nose twitched.

"Before you and the female leave," she added, "come to the cave, then fill your canteens. There's a lake around the side, but do not dare to touch *our* fruit."

Perin just stared at the goblin, wanting to tell her to fuck off, but he held his tongue.

"Are you coming or not?" Lo scowled. "Don't take water as a friendly gesture. I want you to retrieve my gift, not die of thirst."

A scamper of feet came from ahead, and he and Lo slipped forward out of the trees, finding Tavarra rubbing her eyes and frantically searching around.

"What are you doing?" Perin asked.

"I thought you left, you fool!"

Perin thought about his sister, how she'd left Quil behind to complete her task. "There would've been a note if I'd done that."

Her eyes narrowed, and she bared her teeth, a habit she hadn't lost. She looked both fierce and beautiful at the same time.

He angled his gaze away. "But we do need to leave soon."

They gathered their things and followed Lo to the mouth of the first cave. Vaden rested near the entrance, sleeping on his side. On top of him, two smaller goblins slept. Lo rushed forward, swinging her stick back and forth. "The next lot of you I find near him are all dead, you hear me? I already had to get rid of two this morning.”

The small goblins sat up, leaped from Vaden, and scurried off, all while the jovkin remained asleep.

“She’s a bit aggressive, isn’t she?” Perin said, watching Lo strike her stick against the ground and warn the other goblins.

“Just a tad.” Tavarra moved toward Vaden. She pressed her boot against his back and tapped.

He rolled over with a yawn. “Yes?”

“We’re leaving soon.” She knelt beside him. “Have they hurt you?”

“No.” He sat up, his hands still tied behind his back. “Just threats from Lo, but some of the goblins are actually kind.”

Perin arched a brow and stared at the two dead goblin bodies that Lo was pointing at—not sure he would trust any of them. His mouth watered as he stared at the dead bodies. He could already smell the meat through the open wounds.

“Do not eat!” the goblin screamed and jammed her stick at Perin’s leg. “I know you like yours fresh, but these are for him.” She pointed at Vaden. “You two will have to scavenge your own.”

He wanted to tell her to fuck off again but held his tongue once more.

Outside, the fire was already started, and the goblins began cooking.

Lo tossed a charred goblin on the ground between Tavarra and Vaden. She picked it up and did like the night before, except only fed him.

“If we’re not back in a few days,” Tavarra whispered so only Vaden and Perin could hear, “escape back toward the boat and leave. They weren’t smart enough to tie your legs.”

Vaden turned to the side and wiggled his fingers for her to place her hand in his. “Stay safe, my friend. And I will not risk your life for mine.” His eyes then focused on Perin. “You be careful as well.”

“You, too.” Perin stared at the goblins ripping apart meat

and savagely digging in with animalistic sounds. "This looks like a vicious bunch." However, his stomach twitched, and he knew he would need to eat soon.

"Lo, most of all," Vaden grunted.

"What did you say?" the goblin appeared from outside the cave.

"I said you have been kind to keep me alive."

"Only to plump you up," Lo spat. "Now, eat more!" She shoved a blackened arm toward his mouth.

Vaden nodded that it was okay for them to leave, and they returned the motion. Perin and Tavarra trudged around the cave and filled their canteens. She washed out the two glass containers she had—filled with the fairy wings and firefly mixture that no longer worked—to use to hold the lavender liquid.

"Well, I suppose this is your last chance to turn around," Perin said, splashing his face with cool water.

"I'm giving you the same opportunity right now." She smirked.

Tavarra had managed to draw on the hidden strength that had always been hers, the way the water ability had been Rhona's, the way intuition had always been Perin's. Intuition wasn't an ability—he didn't have one of those—but it had always helped him survive.

Before they left, Tavarra snuck four apples from the trees that Lo had warned them not to touch and placed them in her bag. They would all be hers because Perin already knew they would taste like dirt and wouldn't solve his problem.

As they circled around the caves, taking the path leading in the southern direction, the goblins' grumbles drifted further and further away. They entered another forest where unusual hooting sounds and a wild screeching came from some form of creature. Perin's stomach twitched like earlier, but this time an ache accompanied it.

"I have my dagger ready." Tavarra scanned the forest. "I

think we know what your first feast will be.”

As they approached the new territory, she kept her grip on the dagger just as he did his. With the hunger brewing in his stomach, he didn’t know if he would be able to aim true. And that bothered him most of all because he could always do that.

The scent of the forest contained a burnt odor as though the trees were on fire or had been. The trees were charcoal gray with orange leaves and black shriveled fruit. Possibly poisonous.

He warily looked from tree to tree, waiting for a branch or vine to try and capture one of them, but they only moved because of the wind.

Another hoot came from a tree right ahead, and something quickly swung across a vine, growling. It leaped from the vine toward them, and Tavarra didn’t hesitate as she threw the dagger and struck the creature in the head.

“There you go,” Tavarra said as it smacked into a cluster of branches.

As they reached the body, it looked similar to the goblins, except there were curled horns on the side of the head and a wide mouth. Its skin was of a greenish-brown and resembled the texture of a snake.

“You eat. I’m fine,” Tavarra urged, taking one of her stolen apples from her pack, and biting into it. “We still have dried meat that I can eat later.”

Perin scooped the creature up and chewed into its tough flesh along the way. He had waited for the dirt taste to come, but like the goblin, the flavor was almost fascinating, and he held back the animalistic sounds *he* wanted to make. Tavarra didn’t pay any attention as she watched their surroundings and threw her finished apple core to the ground. After Perin ate what he could, his body felt much better.

“It’s strange here,” Tavarra said. “On the other side of Laith, I was never worried about things, even though there are dangers like the jovkins or the volachs. But right now, I’m not entirely sure what to do."

"Whisper would be a good place to start." Perin chuckled softly.

She elbowed him hard.

He was about to make a jest when his eyes focused on something ahead. The darkened area had opened up to something glittery with a light fog rising from the surface. "What is that?" At first, he thought it could already be the lavender liquid, but that wouldn't be right. They hadn't passed through any bramble. And no, it couldn't be that easy—it was something else. Something red and wafting of metal. As they drifted closer and closer, their steps softening to a quiet, the area was not a pure liquid at all, but a sloshy thick texture that spread wide both across and diagonal. The swamp.

The viscous slosh was filled with chunks of *something*. He bit the inside of his cheek to keep from gagging. It smelled rotten, like meat that had been sitting out for days and days. Globs of body parts floated through, bones rested on the surface, and a couple of skulls buoyed up and down.

"Lo didn't mention that the swamp was a bloody mess, only that it belonged to hags," Tavarra muttered.

"What now?" Perin looked for a way to circle around it—there wasn't one.

"We cross."

Perin watched the bones' movement, and something didn't feel right. He stuck out his arm and pulled Tavarra back. "Wait, not yet."

She looked as though she wanted to argue, but she gripped her necklace. He knew she must have had a flashback of what had happened to Eza when Perin had tried to warn the bat to stop before the jovkin killed her.

Perin perked his ears up and listened intently. A slight suction sound came from somewhere beneath the surface of the swamp. He had to pay extra close attention to hear it, or he wouldn't have noticed it at all.

Tavarra pressed her lips together and nodded, hearing it, too.

Silently, Perin raised his sword upward. The spongy liquid swayed as it rippled, something moving beneath. A body sprung up, dripping in red goop. Perin didn't pause and slashed his sword across, decapitating the creature—a hag. The body slumped back into the liquid, and the head rolled to Perin's left. The skin hung loosely on the body and the spine curved, creating a hunch.

Two more creatures drifted forward, slowly peeking their heads above the water. Both with dark, stringy hair cascading past their shoulders and balding in sparse sections. They were too far back for Perin or Tavarra to get to unless they got into the swamp. The hags' large eyes watched them from inside their sunken faces and high cheekbones.

One's gaze found the unattached head beside Perin's foot. "You, human, choose to come near our swamp?" The hag's voice was high-pitched and raspy. "You have already lasted longer than most." The creature tapped its gnarled hands together, its long claws clicking against one another.

"We need to pass," Tavarra said, her voice steady.

"And pass, you shall." The other one—possibly male—cackled and held up a long bony finger. "But I need a body part for now."

"A leg," the hag said, running her forked tongue over her blackened lips.

"No, an arm," the other said, "so she will be able to walk back to us."

"An arm it is," the hag with the forked tongue chirped and slithered forward.

"No one is getting any body parts." Perin leaped into the water, knowing it wasn't that high based on how the swamp only hit the creatures' shoulders. He swung his sword, easily decapitating them both.

"Hurry!" he shouted to Tavarra.

"You're a fool!" Tavarra screamed as she jumped in.

A fool who got the job done. He grabbed her arm and barreled across the swamp. To his left, the suction sound increased, and movement was already coming.

Below the surface, the swamp felt more liquid while the consistency on top was thicker to wade through.

Tavarra pushed herself to the ground on the other side and held down a hand to pull Perin out, just as another hag sprung up. "You do realize you have to come back through if you choose to cross again." Her forked tongue flicked. "We will be waiting."

We? How many of those things were down there?

Blood and guts covered Perin and Tavarra, but there wasn't much he could do about that. Spiderwebs blocked their path, and they both used their swords to slice away the sticky substance to get through the forest.

"Just so you know, I will be bathing in a lake when we're finished with this," Tavarra said in a low voice. "A really, really long bath, then sleep."

"You have such confidence we'll get through this."

"It seems to be a role reversal this time, doesn't it?"

He shook his head, but his lips twitched as he broke through trees folded and twisted in unusual positions with long, dark leaves.

They walked for what seemed like days. Perin felt as though the spiderwebs would never end. With all the webs, he assumed that the spiders were massive, but in fact, it was because there were hundreds and hundreds of tiny ones. He could hear them being crushed beneath his boots, then found their crippled or unmoving white bodies on the ground.

Tavarra ate a piece of dried meat, and he struck what might have been a black deformed rabbit because that was the only thing he'd seen in a bit. The fleshy meat didn't fill his stomach, and the taste was of dirt again.

The suns would set in a little while—his feet hurt, and his

stomach began to ache. Perin pressed his hand to a nearby tree as he stared ahead, the world becoming blurry.

"Where do you want to rest?" Tavarra asked.

"Well," Perin started with sarcasm, "our choices are the spider village that we finally passed to your left or the rocks to your right?" The two dark green rocks came to about his shoulder and were long enough to create a barrier of sorts.

She scowled as though there were some other kind of options.

"Spider it is," he answered for her.

Rolling her eyes, she turned away and took a seat behind the lichen-covered rocks. He plopped down beside her, but not too close.

Before Perin could get comfortable, a stirring came from behind them.

Nineteen

Perin

The sound drew closer from behind the rocks. Perin shot forward to push Tavarra to the ground, protecting her body with his. She looked up at him, her eyes bulging, and clamped her hands tightly to his wrists, about to shove him off. He knew she thought he was going to *eat* her.

He quickly shook his head, then tilted it in the direction of the sounds growing nearer to get a better listen. She squinted her eyes as she cocked her head, and released his hands. The stirring turned into a hobbling of feet clunking at the ground, followed by heavy grunts and breathing. It wasn't just one set of feet, but multiple.

"What shall we feast on tonight?" a rough voice rasped.

"Tasty, tasty, treat it is."

"There hasn't been much of anything tasty since the swamp creatures started to steal our food. Perhaps we should eat them."

"We have. They taste of rot," another answered. "Perhaps we should eat Egor."

"I am right here," a creature who must be Egor replied.

"And you are pathetic and deserve to be eaten indeed."

There was an altercation, and grunts came from what had

to be the athers. Perin and Tavarra both remained perfectly still as the sounds of weapons being whacked and fists punching bodies took place.

A body thumped to the ground, and Perin heard the rustle of it being dragged as the athers scuffled away. Perin perked up his head to see four creatures with sickly green bodies and black hair pulled into low ponytails that reached all the way down to the end of their spines. Some sort of animal fur covered the bottom portion of their body from waist to knee.

Two athers carried the knocked-out creature by his shoulders, his feet dragging the ground while the other hobbled behind them, holding onto a long wooden staff. His weapon was wrapped in braided rope near the top.

Perin wasn't going to take any chances—he lifted a fraction from Tavarra to reach for his sword, and stopped. While going through this unknown place, he didn't want to make things more difficult than they had to be.

"Why didn't you kill them?" Tavarra asked when the athers' sounds had faded into the distance.

"I'm not sure how far away their home is or if they have a whole entire clan like the goblins."

"I think it's safe to say you can get off me now," Tavarra said, lifting her brows.

"Yeah, sorry." Perin nodded, and stood, helping her up. "I think we need to find somewhere else to go."

They walked a little farther out until the flowing of a river drifted through the air. If anything about his day was lucky, this was it. Perin splashed cool water into his mouth, cleansing as much muck away from the swamp as he could.

Tavarra removed her boots first and got right in. He followed her lead and took his off before stepping in next, the water striking at his knees. They tried to get as clean as they could, but the swamp had stained their clothing. When he came out, he was dripping water from his skin and clothing, but he would rather be wet than have a strong scent of old rot that could attract other creatures.

"We're going to have to take shifts resting. Are you up for that?" Tavarra asked, staring down at Perin's hand gripping his abdomen.

"Get some rest first. I'm not even tired." Pain twisted inside his stomach, and if it remained like this, it would be all right. He could deal with a little achiness—he'd put up with more before.

"Me neither. I don't know what we're going to do about food for you. All I've seen for most of this journey are spiders and bugs." She sounded frustrated, and he was, too. About everything.

Tavarra curled up on her side beneath a bush, the branches concealing most of her body, and kept her eyes open. He knew it wasn't because she was frightened, but in case she needed to chain him while figuring out a solution. After a while, her eyes fluttered closed, and she drifted off, most likely not meaning to, but he let her sleep.

Perin drank some more water in hopes that it would expand his stomach, maybe make it stop eating itself because that's what it had to be doing. He distanced himself a good length away from Tavarra and placed his hands in his hair, clamping his jaw tight. The hunger still wasn't there yet, or maybe it was, but his stomach wouldn't stop. While gazing at Tavarra's sleeping form, he thought about how taking a small bite out of her would soothe his pain—he knew that for a fact. He would never do it, but he couldn't help his thoughts from wandering in that direction.

Everything felt unfocused, like it had with the goblins when he'd snapped at her without meaning to. The thought of her scent was becoming all-consuming. He withdrew his dagger and shakily pressed it to his throat in case he got out of control because right then he didn't trust himself. He wouldn't let this festering disease get that way, not around her. Right as he moved forward to wake Tavarra up to watch over him and to chain himself, there was a soft *boom, clack, click*, and something hard thwacked him on the head.

Perin's eyes felt glued shut. He couldn't move. Was he fucking buried again? His lids rose then, and he wasn't surrounded by dirt, but everything was unfocused. His wrists were tied behind his back. A heavy scent filled his nostrils, a delicious one that he craved beyond anything he'd ever imagined.

He knew who he was, he knew what he shouldn't be doing, but the scent caressed his insides as he inhaled. At that moment, he was losing himself as his eyes glazed over, and he snapped his teeth viciously. Shaking his head furiously, he drew himself out of whatever dark place he'd gone to.

A crackling, and loud voices, caught his attention, his hearing finding its balance. His vision cleared and he could see it was still dark outside, but a bright fire was lit wherever he was. For a moment, he thought he was back with the goblins again, but a creature a few heads taller than Perin tossed in part of what looked to be a tree trunk. He resembled the other athers he'd seen earlier but was broader, larger, and stronger.

Perin glanced down at his hip, finding his sword gone. *Of fucking course it is*. He brought his head back and pressed it to a large wooden pole that held him in place. Quietly, he sat and rubbed his tied hands against the pole to try and fray the rope.

"What do we have here?" An ather, with a large, hooked nose, roughly lifted Perin's chin. He leaned in close, sniffing Perin. The scent of whatever was inside the creature permeated the air, teasing him. Perin smelled him right back and snapped his teeth.

The ather jumped away, his dark lips pulling downward before he charged forward and struck Perin across the cheek with his staff. "*We* are the eaters here, not you, human."

Where's Tavarra? a small voice asked at the back of his head. Tavarra. Tavarra. His focus was back, and he searched around the fenced-in area. Tree logs formed a barrier, and no other athers were here besides the two. He couldn't spot her orange hair anywhere. Was she still back by the river? Was she here? Had they *eaten* her? He couldn't ask where she was, because if they hadn't found her, then he couldn't draw that to their attention.

"When's the last time you ate a human?" Perin asked, his cheek on fire from the hit.

"It's been too long since we wrestled one from the swamp creatures," the ather said, his head cocked at an awkward angle.

"One human seems like too little to share."

"It will be sufficient."

He was certain, almost, that they didn't have Tavarra.

From his right, another ather walked in, wearing a fur dress with a strap over one shoulder. She lifted her staff and jabbed him in the stomach, another jab in the head, and one in the arm.

"Stop!" someone shouted. "He will be the higher one's dinner tomorrow night to sacrifice when the moons are full."

As the night went on, Perin's hunger became stronger, unbearable, his appetite increasing, the pain taunting. He knew once he sank his teeth into one of them, it would be vehemently beautiful.

Eventually, they would have to untie him.

Twenty

Tavarra

Tavarra opened her eyes to daylight streaming in. Perin had let her fall asleep—she quickly moved branches of the bush out of the way and sat up before turning to yell at him in a whisper.

When he wasn't there in his spot beside the tree, her heart quieted, then picked up. It was fine. Tavarra didn't need to panic every time he woke up to relieve himself somewhere. No, there wasn't time to wait.

"Perin!" she whisper-shouted.

No answer. The only sounds were the flow of the river and a strange ticking that came from the bugs.

He wouldn't leave her, would he? They couldn't be that far from retrieving the lavender liquid. She could see him possibly leaving her behind on the other side of Laith, but not here, not with those creatures roaming around. Or had he?

The old Tavarra came creeping back in, the one who didn't want to trust anyone after having her heart broken, but she had to trust him.

She stood and scrambled over to the tree where he should have been. His pack rested against the trunk, and his sword lay on the ground. Her eyes widened. Perin would never have left his weapon and gone off somewhere.

"Think, Tavarra. Think."

A large white spider crawled near her boot, and she stomped on it. Against the dirt, she could see footprints—not boots. And something else. It looked as though someone had been dragged—Perin.

Fuck. She wanted to scream, and why hadn't *he*? And she had slept through it all. What a fool she was.

Gathering what she could from his pack, Tavarra placed it in hers, then picked up his sword. Her heart dropped because she didn't know where he had been taken or even if he was still alive. But she was certain from the footprints that it had to be the athers. They were going to be dead. She would rip their heads and arms off today and feel satisfied after she did that and found Perin.

Without making a sound, she followed the footprints that were leading back to the rocks where she and Perin first heard the athers.

"Eza, I know you're not here," Tavarra murmured, clasping her necklace. "But I need you to be around in some sort of form. I need to know what we should do."

Of course, there was no answer. If Eza had been there, she would have been able to scout things out quickly by flapping her wings and flying through the trees. The perfect spy. But now there was no spy, only Tavarra to figure it out on her own.

Her ability—no longer a curse—was with her. "Thank you for this at least," she whispered to the Goddess wherever she was, if she was even real at all.

Being human wasn't perfect, as she once had idealized long ago, but she wouldn't ask for it any other way, and she would never choose to be a sea dweller ever again. When she hadn't had the strength or the speed, she still missed it, just as Rhona had told Tavarra that she had missed her ability when it had been shut off.

The footprints became lighter until she could barely see the bottom of Perin's boots where he had been dragged.

She forced herself to hastily eat a piece of fruit to keep from growing too weak. The heat was making her sweat more than normal.

A sigh escaped her when she came to the rocks—something familiar. Tavarra wasn't sure how much farther she would have to go.

The marks were fading more until there was nothing, but there were puncture marks in the dirt. It had to be the staves. She almost kissed the trees because the small signs weren't leading back to the bloody swamp—she didn't want to have to deal with the hags, too.

Through the forest, thick bushes cluttered the area, and she had to be careful to not make too much noise. Yellow vines fell in every direction, making it seem as if she was walking through a curtain.

Holes. Holes. She needed to find more holes. The ground was much firmer here, and creatures with too many legs scurried up the trees making loud hisses. She let out a frustrated breath and held up her fist, silently cursing every single part of this forsaken place.

At that moment, she didn't care, she punched the air as hard as she could but really wanted to slam her fist into the tree. She imagined Eza swiping her hand across Tavarra's head and telling her to take it easy.

I'm calm now, she told herself and continued forward, the curtains of vines growing less dense. *Cha. Cha. Cha.* Abruptly, Tavarra came to a stop and listened. *Cha. Cha. Cha.* A group chanting in singsong voices came from up ahead. It had to be the athers, unless it was some other cluster of creatures.

Carefully, she made her way in the direction of where the voices were coming from. Around a fat tree, covered in limbs and more limbs, there was some type of village up ahead. The shelters were cylinder-shaped with long sticks on the outside and leafy roofs on top. Broad poles glowed with orange and yellow fire in broad daylight, gray smoke pumping upward.

From her right, an uneven patter sounded. Tavarra shifted to her left and quickly looked in the direction of the noise. Two small ather babes with dark green skin, black hair pulled back, and sharp curled noses, dashed in front of her before coming to a stop.

If they were anything like normal children, she could weasel her way in and gather inside information.

"Hello." Her voice came out a bit too friendly.

In response, both athers growled, then leaped at her with their mouths open wide and teeth bared.

Twenty-One

Perin

There was a demon dwelling inside his body, or was the creature himself? Perin fought his thoughts and focused them on her. *Tavarra.* He desperately needed to know if she was safe.

Throughout the morning, the ghastly creatures hadn't cared much for privacy. They'd fornicated around the fire, creating sounds that sounded more like torture. He'd closed his eyes and counted rabbits as high as he could inside his head, and he couldn't stop himself from imagining sinking his teeth into the fleshy meat of each ather.

Rhona's mother had talked about places where you could go when you died. A very dark spot inside his head thought that maybe this was the miserable place. Maybe he never really woke up after being buried. Maybe he really was dead and nothing here was real—it was all just his imagination.

While staring at the fire, Perin didn't know which was worse, being burned or eaten alive. He hoped they killed him before he could find out.

One ather with thin shoulders and a high forehead picked up a small bone and licked it continuously, even though the meat had been gone for who knows how damn long. He then rolled back and forth in the dirt, naked, as though it was his bath time ritual. *Just spread the dirt instead of the water, and you'll be all clean,* Perin thought sarcastically.

After a while, athers gathered in and out of the dirt pit, taunting him, poking him, running their filthy fingers across his face. As more came in, he couldn't handle the overwhelming odor wafting off them, and his eyes glossed over once more. Each time an ather came close, he snapped at them, hoping for a single taste.

Perin had been tied to the pole for much too long, and the pain inside his stomach now vibrated with something fresh, raw—a pang of hunger so deep that he needed to slice open each creature from throat to navel. Inside there, he would find the tasty treasure he yearned for.

He closed his eyes—everything was a blur as his eyes stayed hazy, but he could smell where every single body stood.

Feasting would be soon, but what they didn't know was that he would be the only one eating.

Twenty-Two

Tavarra

Tavarra shoved the ather babes off her before their teeth could even brush her skin, then took off in a heavy sprint toward the village. She leaped across two logs and had her daggers ready, both swords swinging at her hips. When she chanced a glance over her shoulder at the two beastly creatures, they weren't running after her. They were already distracted by some kind of dark-furred animal that they were ripping apart with their teeth and beating with their fists.

A large fenced-in area sat in the middle of the village with the small shelters surrounding it. She dashed across the tall grass and stopped at a shelter with brown leaves covering the roof. Taking a breath, she placed her back right up against it. The logs were too close together to peer inside with thin rope binding them all together.

The suns would still be up for a while longer, but everything appeared hazy and clouded over, and she wasn't sure if this would make things easier or more difficult. Gripping the necklace around her throat, she hoped that Perin was inside the fenced-in area—alive, not dead—and that Eza's spirit would somehow guide her. But he could easily be somewhere else, or maybe even right inside one of these shelters.

Tavarra had never been in this position before, never really had to save anyone. She was still used to everyone winding up dead. The mer she had shot from the boat wasn't a danger like this—they were tricky but easy to escape from.

She thought about Vaden—if she didn't make it back with the gift for Lo, he would wind up dead, too. Why did everything always have too many paths, too many different choices, too many what ifs? She remembered the story of the creator of Laith, the Goddess who disappeared. *It was your magic that brought Perin back, so where the hell are you? I need you to fix this!* she thought.

The Stone of Desire's words came to mind from the day it had made her human—Tavarra would see more deaths. And she had already. Who would come next?

Releasing Perin's ring and Eza's shell, she crept forward, staying close to the shelter. When she heard the press of heavy steps beating the hardened earth, she darted to a large tree right across from her, ducking behind the trunk.

The bark nipped at her fingers as she buried them against it. Tavarra listened as grunts and staves clacking together passed her. When the sounds faded, she peered around a branch—there were three athers—two males and one female—slipping inside an entrance to the fenced-in area. She could end the life of three, but she questioned how many were inside. The barrier was a good size, forming a square shape.

For now, she placed her pack against the ground behind the tree to make things less bulky, then wandered out and moved quickly to the fence. She planted her face to the poles and peered through the thin slits.

It wasn't three, or six, but maybe thirty creatures within the poled-walls. She pressed her fingers to the bridge of her nose and looked up again to scan inside. When she glanced back up, most were scuttling out and leaving maybe ten inside. *There*, she sucked in a sharp breath when she found Perin tied to a pole. She couldn't see his face clearly, but she had expected him to be slumped over. Instead, he sat on his knees, spine straight, and staring directly at the group of athers.

How am I going to do this? There was no sneaking in, and she was uncertain about their skills with their staves. The one entrance appeared to also be the only exit. There was a high possibility that she could end up dead or with rope binding her wrists like Perin. So she would have to be fast.

The athers were distracted on the other side of the fire as they chanted and roared with someone, possibly a leader, who was speaking.

This was her chance. She swiftly moved around the edge and skirted inside. Perin was right there. She went down to her knees and pressed her body behind his. "Are you all right?" she whispered.

He didn't answer.

A panicked feeling washed over her because he needed to be in a clear state of mind for this. Tavarra angled his face toward hers, and he snapped his teeth. "Shit." She flinched. His eyes were glazed over. But it wasn't just that, there were bruises on his face and a line of dried blood running down his nose and the side of his lip.

Tavarra wanted to murder them all. However, at that moment, they had to get out of there. All she could do was hope for the best. She took Perin's sword and cut through the ropes at his wrists, freeing him.

"We have to leave. The exit is behind you," she whispered, her eyes flicking back and forth between Perin and the athers who had their backs turned.

Perin wouldn't look at her, and he stared straight ahead at the cluster of creatures roaring beside the blaze.

Perspiration formed on her face from the hot flames of the fire. "I'll find you food to eat somewhere outside. Now let's go!"

The fool didn't listen when he rose to his feet. With a

predatory expression and teeth bared, he barreled forward in the direction of one of the athers, knocking a male to the ground. Cocking his head back, Perin drove his teeth straight into the neck of the creature, bright red crimson spraying out.

This caught attention. *Everyone's* attention. One ather with a wide face and a missing nose thwacked Perin in the leg with her staff. Tavarra knew she had to hurry before they killed him—she would just have to find a way to murder them all.

Pulling the two daggers from her waist, she hurled one, striking its mark on the creature without a nose, followed by another ather diving for Perin. Three down, seven more to go. They all looked up at her, not focusing on Perin, who was making a feast of the first one.

They all got their staves ready. No blades.

"Perin!" Tavarra shouted. She found him on his knees, cracking open the skull of the one he had been eating and was now placing pieces of the brain in between his lips. All she could do was scream his name once more. He looked up at her then, his eyes clearing, ruby blood resting on his mouth and chin. "Finally." She slid him his sword, and she didn't know what happened after that because all the athers came toward her, waving their staves. Quickly, Tavarra pulled the sword from her waist. With a hard swing and a jut forward, she stabbed one with a missing ear straight through the chest, the squish echoing.

A staff whacked her in the back, and she could barely breathe. Whirling around, she grabbed the bastard by his neck and twisted it, then threw his dead body across the room.

Another weapon hit Tavarra against the side of her head, and her eyes rolled for a second as she saw stars. As the ather was bringing the staff down again, she kicked the female in the stomach, then stabbed her through the throat. Head spinning, she turned around to prepare herself for the others, but they were all already unflinching on the ground. Except for Perin, his face covered in blood, his sword dripping with crimson.

"I'm not sure when the rest will be back." He wiped the blood from his blade against the fur clothing of one of the athers. "But we need to get going."

Tavarra remembered his glazed-over eyes, the way he yearned for the flesh of the ather.

"No," she said with determination. "You need to eat what you can, so you don't turn into someone who isn't Perin."

"We don't have time for that," he growled.

"We don't have time for you to lose focus, either!" Tavarra retrieved both her daggers from the bodies and brought her sword up. She then slammed it down against an arm, then the other of one of the ather's bodies.

In a hurry, she tossed him the food his body yearned for and held onto the other. "One for now and one for later."

Perin didn't question her as they rushed out from the entrance. She sheathed her sword and snatched up her pack from behind the tree.

"I'll carry the pack for now," she said as they ran through the trees. "I put most of your stuff in here that you could use, and you'll need to save your strength."

"This will set us off a bit," Perin said, nodding, "but we'll have to continue." Then he brought the arm to his lips.———

"Yes, and you better keep up because we're not going to stop for a while," Tavarra said, heading back to the route by the river, but they wouldn't be stopping there for the night this time. "Unless you want me to carry you like a babe again." With a devious smile, she glanced over her shoulder and found him frowning as he ate, but there was a hint of amusement there, too. "Like I said, all you have to do is ask."

"I think I can keep up."

When they jogged past the rocks they had stopped at the day before, Perin called out, "Wait!"

He had gone for longer than she would have expected. "Yes."

"Water…" he grunted the words out.

Tavarra should have offered him that right away, but she had only been thinking about them getting away from the village. His hand held onto the barely eaten limb while the other rested at his stomach.

She knew he was in pain. "Just eat! I'm not one to judge!"

After she handed him the canteen and he drank the water down, he gave it back to her, then did as she said. He grabbed the other arm from her to carry, and she took another fruit from her bag. They ate as they moved.

By the time they reached the river again, he had already tossed the bones and appeared mostly himself. They both chugged their water down and refilled their canteens.

"We shouldn't stay here longer than we have to," Perin said, washing the blood from his face and hands as she did the same.

"I agree. I think if they find you or me again, we'll be killed and eaten on the spot instead of dragged back to their village."

They would have to stop soon, though, because the suns wouldn't be up for much longer. They crossed over the river and headed away from the athers in the southern direction. Tavarra didn't know how far the creatures would go out. Did they normally venture past the river? Would they be able to track them down? They didn't seem to be the brightest of sorts.

"Hey, how are you holding up?" Perin asked.

"About the same as you, surviving," Tavarra said as she slowed down, swiping a branch covered in thorny leaves away from her face. "How are you?"

"Haven't been better."

"You're lying."

Perin chuckled, almost wildly, then he grew serious. "This is the third, no wait, the fourth journey I've been on in my life. And all three have ended in shit. On the first journey, I was smaller, and the Stone never answered me. The second was when my village moved and I ended up taking more abuse from my father. The third was the journey with you where I ended up dead. Oh, and the forth was where I met the Stone once again and Its Shittiness decided to answer me. So I guess, actually, this would make the fifth. And you see how *lovely* it's been."

"Tell me more, why don't you?" Tavarra paused, placed her hands on his shoulders, and smiled. "Would you like me to go over the seven years of awful journeys I've been through? Waking up beside dead bodies isn't a great thing at all."

His expression softened. "I'm so sorry."

"It's not a competition, just that some of us in Laith—you and I—have had to experience worse journeys than most others." She released his shoulders. "And we're not quite finished yet."

"I still wish you'd stayed behind instead of hopping aboard the boat."

"There you go again, trying to make all the decisions."

"What decision do you choose now?"

In front of them, an ear-piercing rumbling stirred, and Tavarra came to an abrupt stop. "Not that one."

Twenty-Three

Perin

Perin lifted his sword, sick of this bullshit of a place. He couldn't catch a break—not with his appetite, not with the pain, not with fucking things continuously popping up.

He was done.

From below the dirt, four creatures sprouted upward, not quite in the same way the Stone of Desire had. But similar. A brown grassy texture covered their backs, making it easy for them to blend in with the ground. Something that looked sticky and wet ran down their bodies.

The creatures were a cross between a bird and a human, with wings as arms. On their faces rested a beak covered in grass, and their eyes the shade of blood. Their skin had a hue that matched the dirt, and they even moved like humans, except for their necks, which bobbed back and forth as they hissed. One released its dark tongue and it struck Perin across the neck. A scalding sensation ran up his skin as though it was on fire.

"Watch out!" he yelled to Tavarra. "Their tongues burn."

Perin leaped forward and swung his sword, thinking it would be an easy task to remove the creature's head. The bird-thing dodged the blade and kicked Perin in the chest with its leg. His back slammed into the trunk of a tree. The creature moved toward him, flapping its grassy wings with a deep and booming whistling screech. Perin glanced at Tavarra, who had pounced on one and taken it to the ground, killed it, and was getting back on her feet.

Perin pushed forward and rammed the bird back with his boot, then shoved his sword straight through its chest. He ripped his sword out, and the creature slumped to the ground, a thick brown dirt texture oozed out and clung to his weapon. These wouldn't sate his appetite, even if he were hungry.

Tavarra flipped one to its back and stabbed the creature in the head while the last moved for Perin. He hurled his sword at the perfect angle, and it sliced right through the creature's ribcage, heart, and poked out from its back.

Eyeing the area, he retrieved his sword. "Keep a lookout."

Nothing else shifted from the ground, and he made sure to be careful with his steps as they moved forward. Then the world around him seemed to shrink, and he thought it was something going on with his sight, but it wasn't. It was as though the trees were getting pushed closer together, thorns becoming denser. Everything felt too overcrowded—there was an overwhelming amount of foliage. He could barely walk through any of it.

Across the ground, silver thorns protruded from all angles on top of charcoal gray limbs. Everywhere. "This has to be the bramble, which means the lake must be through here." His heart pumped with what could only be hope. He didn't know if he should dare hope, though, so he pressed the emotion back.

Above him, branches of thorns created a cloak over them. Even if he was a bird, he wouldn't be able to fly his way out unless he went in the direction he'd come… Maybe. But he had no wings of any kind, only two arms that could swing a sword.

His gaze narrowed at a yellow fluid that dripped out from the tips of each of the silver thorns. Tavarra's shoulder was about to brush one, and he pulled her back. "Wait! What is that?"

Tavarra studied it and reached the tip of her sword forward to make contact with the liquid. The metal of her sword sizzled and disintegrated, a small hole left behind on the blade.

"This creates a challenge to get to the lake then," Perin stated the obvious, puckering his lips and shaking his head. Again, his eyes flicked to the top of the bramble, the ground, the sides.

"We'll have to suck in and be as careful as possible," Tavarra said.

Perin was about to nod until he saw something in his peripheral made of white and bone with a staff at its side. "Like that skeleton over there?"

"What skeleton?"

He pointed his sword in the direction of the one who would stay nameless. It looked to be one of the athers' remains.

"This just means we have to be *extra* careful." She paused. "And don't even ask me to turn around and wait outside the bramble."

That was what he was going to do, but there were plenty of dangers out there, too. It was better if she went with him.

Closing his eyes, Perin sucked in air and swiveled as best he could. He sensed his heart and lungs wanting to buckle on him when a poisonous drop from one of the thorns was too close for comfort from touching his eyeball. The tip of another brushed his pants, and he could hear the sizzle of the cloth being burned away, but he didn't glance down.

Using his sword, he sliced several thorns away. The thought occurred to him that this might have been why the athers hadn't been able to get through. While a staff was an excellent weapon, it wasn't made for cutting. He chopped more and more bramble, making sure to not press his sword near the poison, only the place where the thorns connected to the branches.

At the front was a spot resembling a small opening. Tavarra was still right behind him, and he dipped down so he could crawl through.

He barely had time to look at the scenery or the lake in front of him when a gasp came from behind him.

Whirling around, he found Tavarra swiveling through the space with a determined and slightly angry expression.

"What is it?" he asked.

"Something sizzling on my pack," she said, standing up and peering back at it. "I think it's my hair."

Sure enough, a few orange locks had broken off. He pushed them away with his blade, and they glided to the ground.

"You can bury them if you wish." He gave a casual shrug.

"I can bury you!" She pointed a finger at his chest.

"Been there, done that," he said playfully.

If a glare could kill, hers would have struck him dead. Again.

Grabbing her shoulders, he turned her around to face the lake. It was one of the most brilliant colors he'd ever seen with a rich waterfall centered in between a mountain of rocks, trickling down the effervescent liquid. The water glistened a soft lavender, with a glittering sheen.

Things in Laith could always be tricky, like the brambles they'd just passed through. Perin picked up a small gray pebble and tossed it into the lake to see if it would melt. The sound made a soft plinking noise but didn't sizzle.

Tavarra removed the pack, and he opened it to find the two empty vials and filled them with the water—one for the Stone and the other for Lo. The liquid brushed his palms, and a tingling sensation crawled up his arm as though it was trying to soothe him. He didn't like the liquid touch and shook his arm out as he capped the water, then placed the vials back into Tavarra's pack.

"We have two options," she said, gazing up at the sky. "Go

back now, or my preference—waiting until morning.”

His hunger was satiated from his earlier meal, and from staring up at the dimming sky, they would need to spend the night here. Bramble encircled the area, so nothing could get in except the way they'd come. He believed this would be the safest place to stay, and he didn't think going through the forest at night was smart.

“We can stay the night here,” he finally said.

“All right, we'll head out right at dawn then, and I'll keep watch.” Tavarra stared up at the waterfall. “I won't fall asleep this time.”

“I don't think I'd be able to sleep, even if I wanted to.” Quietly, he sat down beside her, his muscles and face aching. It was as if he couldn't think about it while he moved, but now that he was finally getting a break, it was all he could focus on.

Together they both looked up at the night sky.

“Do you think we could drink the water from there?” she asked, crinkling her nose. “It looks almost too beautiful.”

“I wouldn't dare to try, even if I was told I could.”

After a while, Tavarra placed her hands on the ground and propped her legs out, the moon highlighting her hair, becoming a beacon for him.

Once again, he couldn't help but hone in on her scent, and he knew the need to feed was somewhere hidden … for the time being. But for how long?

What he needed was a distraction, to not think, to not feel. “So tell me something about you that I don't already know.”

Tavarra tapped a finger against her lower lip. “Okay, well, the goddess in the story I told you about—the creator—I always wanted to be her when I was smaller. She had the power to do anything.”

“But it was all stripped away.”

“Because of love,” she said. “At the beginning, when I became the beast, when I was cursed, I felt as if I had become her. Being betrayed, the love not really being love. I don't know."

"Do you still believe in love?" he asked, not meeting her gaze, yet yearning to, while wanting to rest his palm against her cheek. He didn't. Instead, he kept his hands against the dirt.

"I don't know… I loved Nezarra. I loved Eza." She paused. "What about you?"

Perin didn't quite know what love was. He had no idea how long it took to form that kind of bond with someone. Was it years? Months? Weeks? Days? Never? "I've only ever loved my sister. I loved the image of my mother, but I never knew her. If anything, she may have been just as terrible as my father. But we'll never know now, will we?"

"So there were never any other women in your village who you … fancied?" Tavarra asked, and he knew she was studying him.

He thought about her question, really thought about it. Had he? "No."

"You never once found anyone attractive … ever?" She sounded skeptical, but it was the truth.

"No."

"Oh." Her tone sounded like a shrug, and he couldn't leave it at that.

"What?"

"Nothing… It's just interesting, is all."

"And you?" Perin prodded. "Besides the man who I would like to kill."

Blowing out a breath of air, she reclined her head back. "Below the sea, it was all in fun. Sometimes it was a female, sometimes a male. It was always a distraction from where I really wanted to be. But no love. Only the one time with Brice, or so I thought."

"Oh." It was his turn to say the word because his lack of experience had him irked. Sure, he had found release from his frustrations by using his hand … a lot, but what he knew about a woman's body was nothing. It was lacking. He was completely and utterly pitiful. When he thought about the one kiss shared between them, he wasn't even fucking sure if he'd done that right.

"What?" And it was her turn to say *that* word.

"I just—" A heavy pain hit his stomach, cutting him off. He rolled to his side, pulling his knees up to his chest. It was a position he was getting all too familiar with.

A hand came down on his arm. "Do you need anything?"

"No, I'm not hungry. But the pain is there," he said through gritted teeth.

She moved to his other side and lay down face to face beside him, pressing a hand to his cheek. "If you snap at me again, I promise I'll snap at you right back." When he didn't say anything, she continued, "It was only a jest, Perin. Just keep talking to me or perhaps try to sleep, whichever will get you to not think about this for now."

"Tell me another one of your stories."

She pinched her lips together, as though in thought, before giving him a slight nod. "There once was a sea dweller who was cursed as a werewolf and a man helped to save her, even though he wasn't there to see her outcome. In return, the man was cursed as a zombie, and this time, the woman was there to return the favor. But she would be there for the entire journey. No matter what. Even when he was hungry, even when he was in pain, even if he was angry, or sad, or pitifully frowny. She had called him 'fool' numerous times, but he wasn't really a fool, even though he could be foolish at times. But so could she." Tavarra pressed her index and middle finger to his eyelids and drew them shut, her salty scent lingering.

Perin's stomach still thumped with dull aches, but somehow, he fell asleep through it and knew that his heart was feeling something it never had before.

Twenty-Four

Tavarra

Tavarra hadn't slept, not a single wink. She had remembered the night before all too well and didn't want to have to scavenge the area to locate Perin again. Because this time, she might not find him alive—or at all.

Throughout the night, and even now, his knees stayed tucked to his chest with one arm clamped around his middle. It was more than him needing to eat.

Each time he ate, the meat might have slowed down whatever was going on inside of him, but Rhona's mother's blade had punctured him in the exact spot he was clutching. She wondered if he was rotting from the inside out, and she wasn't sure if eating a mountain of flesh would ever satisfy what was going on inside him.

That's why they needed to hurry to the Stone, and she hoped it would choose to save him.

The world was so dark, still cloaked in black, but Tavarra would have to wake him soon. She was only waiting for the rise of the suns to take the moons' place. Her strength may have returned, but her eyesight waned and lacked any resemblance of what she once had. But even if she did have it, she wouldn't have risked traveling back with Perin because his sight, like all humans, was never great in the dark.

Halfway, she told herself. Even though they both looked like death, they had made it this far. She honestly didn't know if they could get to the boat again, but she would keep telling herself, and him, that they would.

The hint of yellow rose up, lighting the pink sky to a fiery hue by creating a fluorescent orange for several moments. She shook Perin's broad shoulder. "Come on, we need to go ahead and leave."

His blue eyes flew open, and his stare was glazed over for a moment, then it settled on her, softening.

"Ready?" she asked.

Pushing himself to sit, Perin rubbed a hand down his tired face, then stood. "Yeah, let's do this."

"You need something to eat," Tavarra said, and it wasn't a question—she knew he did.

"Yes."

"Then let's see what we can find on the way back." Most of the things they had seen so far, she didn't care if they wound up dead. Almost everything they had encountered in Kova wanted the same thing from them—to eat them to their bones.

Before she entered the bramble, Perin lifted his shirt a little, and she caught a glimpse of the scab where Rhona's mother had stabbed him. A sinking feeling washed over her. "Has it changed at all since you first woke?"

Perin shook his head. "The scab still looks the same."

Strange… "Let's just hurry." She flicked her eyes to the closed-in twisted bramble in front of her, wishing Eza was there to guide them the rest of the way back.

Just go the way you came, the bat would have said. *You'll be fine, and if you end up dead? Well, it was worth the risk, right?*

Whatever you say, Eza. Tavarra took a breath and entered the bramble first this time, finding it a little less challenging to push through. One of the thorns got extra close to the tip of her nose, and she twisted her head a little to avoid the burn. Another leaked its yellow liquid and scorched a small hole in her tunic.

Tavarra silently cursed inside her head, because she knew if she said anything, her body would twist in a way to where another thorn near her neck could touch. Then she might very well end up becoming like the skeleton resting inside the bramble. She considered herself a fool right now, but she was growing used to making the wrong choices. Even though she had made a lot of right ones recently—by coming here to help Perin. Nezarra would have told her not to, and that it was a mistake, but Eza would have said that this man needed Tavarra's help.

Behind her, Perin bent and moved his large muscular body in ways that could have only been learned from his skilled sword fighting. Underwater, movements were much easier to stop and prevent oneself from falling. If she fell here, she wouldn't be able to catch herself without making contact with a silver thorn.

Finally, she stepped out from the bramble and turned to grab Perin's hand, quickly pulling him out a bit too hard. They stumbled back into a tree, where his body pressed against hers.

They both stayed there for a moment too long, both breathing hard, then Perin took a deep inhale, and his eyes fluttered shut.

"Perin," she whisper-shouted to snap him out of it.

He blinked rapidly and took a step back.

"You have to try not to *smell* me."

"I'm trying my damned hardest, Tavarra." He looked defeated, ashamed.

"All right, let's see what we can find." She tapped his cheeks twice. "But you have to hold out until we can get back through those trees."

"Just let me go first because I don't completely trust myself walking behind you." He was being honest, and that was what they both needed to get through this.

"That's fine, but let me know if you need to switch." Tavarra looked around. "We can easily head back north, but the bloody swamp will be our main challenge." She didn't want to think about having to get back in there just yet.

They trudged through the forest and only encountered the bodies of the grassy creatures that resembled birds and humans. But they weren't lying where Tavarra and Perin had left them, the bodies were now wrapped in spider silk with hundreds and hundreds of white spiders crawling all over them.

A rustling came from a bush ahead, and Tavarra pulled out her dagger. She moved the limb back and a creature resembling a squirrel, without fur and covered in wrinkled skin, growled at her. With her dagger, she sliced the air, missing it as the creature vanished down a hole.

Slumping her shoulders, she turned to Perin. "You wouldn't have wanted to eat that thing anyway."

"I don't think the small creatures are holding me over."

Tavarra tugged a piece of dried meat out from her pack and ate it while Perin moved beside her and surveyed the area.

The trickling sound of the river seemed to be calling her as they drew closer. She remembered Perin being taken from there, so she was careful to study the foliage, but she should have been looking upward. Something leaped from a tree directly in front of her, and before Tavarra had time to think, Perin pulled her out of the way.

He plunged his sword into an ather's middle right as another one fell from the branches. She slammed her dagger into its skull and hurriedly looked up to see several more swinging from branch to branch. She prepared to fling her dagger up because the aim was perfect, but one plopped down behind her. Tavarra whirled around and stabbed the bastard between the eyes before he could strike her with his staff.

Two more flung themselves in front of Perin, and each

held a staff at his throat, but that didn't stop him as he sliced through one's abdomen. Tavarra charged forward and yanked the other ather to the ground, holding it down. "How many of you are there?"

The creature spat, and the saliva missed her face. She slit the female's throat.

Cocking his head, sprayed with ather blood, Perin listened. "I think we're in the clear for now, but we better hurry."

"How do you know?" Tavarra wondered how he could tell because there were so many sounds going on. Insects, swishing of leaves, and clacking of something.

"They make a distinct sound," Perin said, cleaning off his sword.

"I didn't hear anything besides a lot of rustling." She hurried and pulled out their canteens for them to drink and refill.

"Boom, clack, click." He added the sound effects with his hands, then took his canteen from her to drink.

"Perhaps I may have heard that. I don't know." She downed her water.

"Another lesson I need to teach you then."

"I'm not sure that's a skill that can be learned." Tavarra dipped her canteen into the river, letting the water slide inside.

"Anything can be learned." Perin knelt beside her and did the same. "Maybe not mastered, but learned."

"Are you saying I can't master the ather sounds?" she asked, sarcasm lacing her tone.

"Oh, no." He smirked. "I think you can be a master at whatever you wish."

"Correct answer." She smiled and withdrew her sword, glancing down at the dead bodies. "Now, more importantly, leg or arm?"

"Surprise me."

She stared at the mud-covered feet, then the arms. The feet didn't look appetizing for anyone. Actually, none of the body did, but they would make do. She knew what the choice would be as she brought her blade down and cut off the two arms. It had helped Perin the day before, so she handed him a bloody appendage while she held the other.

"You know I can take body parts for myself." Perin stared down at the arm in his palms. "You don't have to keep doing it."

She placed a hand on his shoulder. "Just *eat* it. You need to learn that others can help take care of you, too. You don't have to be the only one to try and take care of everything. Now let's go."

As Perin ate, they didn't walk at a leisurely pace, they hurried. Tavarra moved a branch out of the way, and her gaze landed on the familiar large rocks. Perin stopped and listened closely—she did the same—not hearing the three sounds he had mentioned to her.

When Perin tosssed the bone of the ather down, she handed him the other arm. He needed to fill himself as much as he could.

While Perin ate, they darted through the trees that had already been draped in new spider silk. She sliced at it as the white spiders seemed to watch but not attack. *They can have the ather bodies that we killed as a gift.*

This was a sign that they weren't too dreadfully far from the swamp.

Good.

Tavarra wiped the sweat from her forehead as she continued on, and they kept their voices completely silent, listening to the ticking of bugs. She wondered after this was over how she would feel. With everything going on, she hadn't had enough time to focus on her melancholy, or her anger, or anything else but this specific task. Maybe this was what she needed to help herself truly heal.

It felt like it took forever to get past all the webbed trees, but they finally did. Dark blue flowers with black centers twisted their heads as they passed. Up ahead, the swamp neared, a fog wafted up from the bloody sludge, making it harder for her to see. When she looked at Perin, he put a finger to his lips. Tavarra nodded in agreement and started forward, careful with each step, using quiet precision.

He moved forward and leaned right up to her, cupping his mouth with his hands and placing them gently around her ear. She couldn't help but focus on the soft feeling of his warm breath, tickling her skin.

"There's no point in trying to stand around at the swamp for them to take notice," he whispered. "We're going to go right in and move to the other side."

All right, she mouthed. His sword was already in his hands, and she clenched her daggers in her own. As they drew closer to the fog, the odor hit her nostrils when they stepped toward a tree near the swamp. The smell was strong, metallic, and rotten—she covered her nose with her inner elbow for a moment to block out the overwhelming scent. Bones floated across the surface and tiny bubbles drifted upward.

Perin held his hand up with three fingers in front of her face.

She blinked in understanding.

He ticked off one, two, three, then they both ran for it. She leaped into the sloshy scarlet texture, her feet planting into the squishy bottom. Almost immediately, the gaunt hags swarmed to the surface—at least three for now. A hag sprung up, almost completely bald with only a few dark locks of hair dangling. Tavarra spread her arms in an X and released them, making two slices against the creature's neck. Hot blood sprayed her face.

In front of her, Perin wrestled with the other two. As she moved forward to help him, another one grabbed Tavarra from behind and dragged her down below the surface. She twisted and fought. Even with her strength, it was hard to get the thing off her—its arms constricted her throat and the legs wrapped around her waist too tightly.

Tavarra moved her hands to grab the hag's head and flip it from her body—a sting so heavy ran down her hands, no, her fingers. The pain deepened, and she wanted to scream with fury.

Despite her anger and the throbbing in her fingers, Tavarra held no fear. She head-butted the hag, but it did not affect the release. The rotten taste of the swamp filled her mouth and nose—she needed air. Her unhurt hand clutched the dagger, then slammed the weapon into whatever part of the ghoulish thing she could. The creature released her a fraction, leaving Tavarra enough space to whirl around so that they were face to face in some sort of twisted embrace. Tavarra pushed her hands against the bony chest and the hag retreated, causing her fingers to radiate. She was blind in the murky liquid, and her eyes burned, but she found the creature's head and twisted it to the side, hearing the loud sound, even underneath the sludge.

Hastily, she burst through the surface, her eyes unable to focus. Then she found Perin plunging his sword through a hag's head.

She breathed hard and rushed as fast as she could to the other side.

He turned to look at her as he approached the edge of the swamp, not appearing the least bit tired, but worried.

"How many did you kill?" she asked, hurrying to catch up, hoping the hags were all dead.

"Ten," he said, lifting her, so she fell to the grass.

Ten? She helped tug him out of the swamp as more heads bobbled up from the depths, only their eyes visible. Not a single one of them crept forward.

When she released her hold on his arm, a sharp pain shot through her hand, and she gasped, moving farther away from the swamp before dropping to her knees.

"What happened?" Perin searched her face, his eyes

worried.

Her adrenaline rush had vanished. Tavarra looked down at her shaking left hand—the tips of her middle and ring finger were both gone, her blood mixing with the uncleanliness of the swamp.

"Fuck!" Perin shouted. "I should have helped you."

"You were," she said, chest heaving. "With the *ten* you slaughtered."

"Don't try to be funny right now."

"Don't try to be serious right now," she bit back. Her hand was still there—it had only been small bites, not all of the two fingers.

"You're missing parts of your fingers, and the wounds are covered in the filth of the swamp!" With precision, he gathered sticks and leaves from the ground and hurried to start a small fire.

"What are you doing?" Tavarra asked.

"I'm going to stop the bleeding, and hopefully, you won't get an infection." Perin poured water from her canteen, removing the swamp filth from her trembling hand. He then lifted his dagger to the flames, the end of the blade glowing.

"I can do it," Tavarra said, taking the hot weapon from his hand. If she could deal with everything that had happened so far, she could do this herself. Without even shaking, she put the dagger to her fingers and held back the scream that wanted to find its way out. Her eyelids fluttered, and she slipped away into darkness.

Twenty-Five

Perin

The body was a machine like no other, one Perin wished he could have built as a child and constructed a new one for himself, but that was always impossible.

Perin was tired. He'd never been this tired in his entire life. Not after being cut over and over again by his father, not when hunting, not when fighting the infection from Rhona's blade to his leg, not when his own mind wanted to battle him.

He stared down at Tavarra, cradling her close, walking toward the goblin village.

After she passed out, he didn't even try to wake her, just placed the pack on his back and scooped her up. Those fuckers had taken two of her fingers right above the knuckles, and he wanted to run his blade through the rest of them. But there was no time for that.

Tavarra shifted in his arms, and her dark eyes met his. "What are you doing!" she shouted and leaped from his arms, then shook her hand out. "Ow!"

"It's going to hurt for a while."

"I have some healing ointment in my pack somewhere," she said. "And don't change the subject! You were carrying me when I told you not to waste your strength."

"I'm not going to apologize." Perin unshouldered the pack and opened it to find the ointment. At the bottom of the bag was a small jar. He snatched it out and unscrewed the lid, then dipped a finger inside. "Let me see your hand."

Pursing her lips, Tavarra hesitated before sticking out her wounded fingers. Quietly, he spread a generous amount on both her bloody digits. He wouldn't have even noticed her uneasiness except for the vein along the side of her throat throbbing too quickly.

"Thank you," Tavarra whispered, as though it was hard for her to say. Without another word, she took the pack from him and placed it on her back. He knew if he refused, she would pull out her blade and demand to do it, so he didn't argue.

They trudged through the forest until they could see the outline of the caves. A part of him wasn't fully sure if Vaden would be alive, and if he wasn't, then Perin would have to gut as many goblins as possible.

"Perin?" Tavarra interrupted his thoughts.

"Yeah?"

"You're frowning more than usual. Do you need something to eat already?"

"I'll be fine," he said as they drew closer into the village. The dark gray smoke from the goblin fire rose upward.

Tavarra placed a hand on his arm, stopping him. "That's not the same as *is* fine."

He rubbed a filthy hand along the back of his neck. "I know, but really, I'm still not hungry." What really made him uneasy was not knowing when the craving would stir again.

"Why won't you look at me?" she asked softly.

"Because." Because he wanted his fucking heart to one day belong to her. Because he wanted her heart to belong to him. Because he could destroy that heart at the same time by feasting on it.

From his peripheral, Perin could see a large stick coming to whack him in the side. He raised his sword and brought it down on the stick, knocking it from Lo's hands. "I wouldn't do that."

Lo looked between Perin and Tavarra with her teeth bared and claws ready to slash at him. "You two were trying to sneak away without finishing the barter."

"Is Vaden still safe?" Tavarra asked, ignoring Lo's asinine comment, hand fisting her dagger.

"Keep calm." Lo craned her neck over her shoulder. "The sacrifice is still alive. He has become quite the entertainment."

Perin closed his eyes in order to not grow frustrated. "Take us to him, then we'll give you the lavender."

"If you tell lies, human, we will take your tongue first." She turned around and hobbled toward the fire.

Lo didn't question the swamp filth staining their clothing and coating their skin as they followed her to Vaden.

At the entrance to the cave, the heat from the fire warmed Perin. The goblins outside watched Perin and Tavarra while others cackled to themselves. Lo went inside and came out a few moments later with Vaden and four other goblins guarding him.

When Vaden lifted his chin, his gaze met Perin's first, and he smiled. "I knew you two would survive." He appeared fed and not the least bit tired.

Tavarra retrieved one of the bottled vials of the lavender water and held it up. "Free him."

Lo nodded and a goblin, with one shoulder larger than the other, bit at the rope, then untied Vaden's wrists.

Perin carefully watched, not trusting a single goblin around as Tavarra handed Lo the vial. The goblin grinned, showing her disintegrating teeth. "You three can get cleaned up and leave in the morning, but you might want to start running now because once the suns go down, our bargain is over."

"What?" Tavarra seethed while Vaden stopped.

Perin raised his sword, knowing something like this would

happen. "Let's go."

"Oh, look." Lo smiled viciously. "The suns are starting to set now."

"Run!" Tavarra and Perin shouted to one another at the same time.

"That little bitch," Tavarra spat over and over as they took off running toward the boat.

Perin hadn't forgotten the trees, the vines, or the birds as he led the way. The trees creaked and groaned. A vine shot out, and he sliced it before it even got close. Tavarra ripped one as it came down like a whip and popped Vaden on the back.

The birds flapped their wings and made their strange noises, and as the light faded little by little, their eyes began to glow.

"Can you two run any faster?" Tavarra yelled when she was the first to strike the sand and stopped.

"What?" Perin said, and he clutched his stomach when a sharp ache hit it. *This isn't the time.*

Then he saw it.

Vaden froze beside them. "The sand is *moving.*"

"It did that before when I was smaller."

Human, something seemed to whisper from behind him up in the trees.

"Ignore it," Tavarra said.

"You heard it?" Vaden asked.

"I think we're all hearing different things from them. But that's not our problem, this is." She pointed just ahead.

Their boat was on a sand wave and collided with the water. He watched as it started to sail away.

"I don't know how to swim." Vaden's voice was high and his eyes wide.

"Well, you better fucking learn," Perin said and took off running toward the boat at the same time the other two did.

A wave of sand collided with Perin's back, knocking him

to the ground. He spat out the gritty texture and tried to barrel forward when another grainy wave hit. From behind, in the distance, he could hear the clamoring sounds of the goblins, and he wanted to chuck his sword at something.

When he rose, Perin found Vaden shoulder-deep in water, trying to get to the boat. *He can't walk to the fucking boat!*

"Perin!" Tavarra screamed.

"I'm here!"

She was already feet deep in the water.

"Go!" Perin demanded, just as another sandy wave pushed him into the water. He came up coughing and a spear landed beside him—from a goblin. Releasing a groan, he kicked his legs as he stroked his way to the boat. Tavarra was up ahead, but he could barely see anything else.

After swimming for what felt like forever, he reached the boat.

"We're already up here," Tavarra called down.

Perin grasped the rope and pulled himself up, letting his body collapse onto the deck. He turned his head to Vaden, who was already up and steering. "Thought you couldn't swim."

"Tavarra tugged me most of the way," he said, adjusting the helm.

"Where is she?"

As if in answer, she appeared on deck with two of the blankets from down below. She tossed him one.

He averted his gaze as she undressed, but he couldn't help glancing at her curves before staring down again as she wrapped her body in one of the blankets.

He was a fool. A fool who remained sitting there, shivering in wet clothing. Turning away from them—from her—Perin stripped out from his clothes and placed the blanket around him.

A hard cramp pulsed through his stomach, and he took a seat to prevent himself from falling over.

"Perin?" she asked, concerned.

When he heard his name roll out from between Tavarra's lips, he couldn't even look at her. He'd been a fool—as she would have said—this entire time. He was tired, and he couldn't even stop using that word. He repeated it like a mantra over and over again in his head, because if he didn't, the new word would be *famished*, and he didn't want to think about that word, because if he did, then he would look to Tavarra. Her scent was already overwhelming—in an intoxicating way, making his eyelids flutter.

"I'm fine," he said, collapsing to his side, grasping his stomach.

Twenty-Six

Tavarra

A wave hit the boat, and Tavarra stumbled while moving toward Perin to help him. A sharp pain struck Tavarra's left hand when she grabbed Perin's arm and rolled him to his back. The hag hadn't gotten the whole of her fingers, but the injury still burned right then as though the creature had. The throb pulsated like nothing else she had ever felt.

Perin's eyes were tightly shut, and she could see lines at the corners of his lids. The one between his brows deepened, and his jaw clamped shut.

Tavarra placed her hands on his shoulders, prepared for him if he snapped his teeth at her. "Perin!"

"It hurts." He breathed. "My stomach."

Vaden came near Perin's feet and placed the lantern beside her. "He needs to eat something."

Tavarra frantically scanned the deck, knowing there would be nothing. Behind her, Kova was already too far, and it wasn't as if they could easily pluck a goblin off the shore while the others let them do it.

There was nothing. He couldn't eat the fruit or the dried meat or even a fish. Vaden looked as if he was going to offer his arm again. Tavarra stared down at her throbbing hand and thought of an idea that could possibly hold him over, but she didn't know if it would.

Taking her dagger from her wet pants, she pressed it into the palm of her hand until scarlet bloomed.

"What are you trying to do?" Vaden asked, shaking his head. "That isn't smart."

"It's his only option right now." She brought her hand near Perin's face.

His eyes shot open, and he shifted away. "What are you doing?" he growled.

With her strength, Tavarra held his chest down in case his eyes glazed over. "Just drink it for now."

"Remember when I told you about vampires at Lana's house?" His nostrils flared heavily. "That's not what I am."

"I still don't quite know what that is, besides you mentioning that they have fangs, drink blood, and never grow old."

"Exactly." Perin dropped the back of his head against the deck and didn't look at her or Vaden. "That's not what I am. I'm not immortal. I don't have fangs. And I need something more than blood to survive."

"I don't care!" she shot back. "You don't know everything! Now try it!" She shoved her hand in his face.

His gaze met hers then, in a battle that she would beat him at. Without blinking, or removing his stare, he clenched his jaw and grasped her wrist. Almost tenderly, he pressed her hand to his lips. As he began to drink, she could feel the soft suction.

When his teeth started to clamp down, she took her hand away. "Okay, that's enough for now. Do you feel better at all?"

"No. Yes. I don't know." Perin sat up and wiped his mouth. "The ache is still there, but it doesn't feel like death anymore."

"That's good," Tavarra said. "So we have a solution to hold you over until we get to shore."

"No, we're not doing that again." He adjusted the blanket and picked up his wet clothing and weapons. "I'm going to go below deck."

Tavarra didn't argue back as he walked away. But she hated seeing him like this. His shoulders and chin were always high and steady, determined, but at that moment, they were slumped as though he had given up on everything. She knew that feeling all too well. Perin shouldn't be like that, though.

Vaden hadn't said another word, only watched with an unreadable expression.

"Yes?" Tavarra finally said since she knew he had something he wanted to share but wasn't willing to just say it.

The jovkin's golden eyes flickered against the lantern's light. "Will you be all right going with him to the Stone when we get back?"

"We'll be fine," she said in a hurry.

"I don't mean Perin, I mean *you*."

What was he talking about? Then something in his expression changed into one of concern, and it hit her then that Vaden wouldn't be going. "Where are you going?"

"While you two were gone, I sat in the cave most of the time, thinking about Aubrey." He paused and took a breath. "There's something I need to take care of … for her."

"But you said you had nowhere to go," Tavarra snapped.

"At that moment, it was true. I didn't even know if I ever could go back, but I now feel like I can."

"You felt bad for me, is that it?" Tavarra was tired of letting someone in, only for them to leave.

"You looked as though you needed a friend." He smiled. "And maybe I needed one, too."

"Is that what we are?"

"I would say so." Vaden must have noticed her tightened fists. "We aren't ever not going to see each other again, Tavarra. You have your strength back, I've seen that. And you don't need me to help you get Perin to the Stone of Desire."

He placed a hand on her shoulder, and for the first time since Eza died, she felt that she could be okay, depending on herself.

Tavarra flexed her fingers, and the pain shot back.

Vaden's gaze shifted down, and his lips parted. "What happened to your hand?"

"Just a small altercation. I'll be okay." She smiled and went to her pack to reapply the healing ointment. "I'm going to go below deck to check on Perin."

"Perhaps you should let him stay by himself until we get to shore."

"No."

"I'm only looking out for you both."

"I know." With those final words, Tavarra turned around and headed down the ladder, smoothing the ointment over her fingertips, the throbbing already lessening.

Down below, Tavarra expected to find Perin asleep—instead, he sat propped against the wall with a lantern flickering beside him.

"You never listen." He shook his head.

"Seems I had to tell you the same thing before." She sat down next to him with her dagger by her side. She was careful, not stupid. And if something did happen, she knew where to stab without it being detrimental to Perin's life.

The rest of the night, neither of them spoke, and they both stared out the window into the night at the silvery glow of the moons until they could stay awake no longer.

As soon as dawn came, Tavarra left Perin asleep to gather fish from the ocean. Vaden and Tavarra ate what they could. She brought Perin down a fish to try again just in case. He ate it and complained of it tasting like dirt. But she knew he finished the whole thing because she had brought it, though he could have stopped at one bite.

Perin continued to spend most of his time below deck while she stayed above, demanding the boat go faster. It didn't listen to her.

"Vaden, why won't the sea just listen to me and get us there quicker?"

"I think the sea has blessed us by keeping the mer away."

Tavarra bit her tongue because that was true.

The night had fallen into its repetitive cycle, and she went downstairs to check on Perin, finding him shivering on his side. He opened his eyes—they weren't glazed, but she could tell he was having a hard time focusing them.

With her dagger, she bit the tip into her palm and let the crimson blossom to the surface. "Look at me. Does it hurt?"

"No," Perin said. But she believed his answer to be a lie. And it was, because he knew what she was doing.

"Does it hurt?" she asked again.

"Yes," he whispered. "It's hard to focus on anything else."

Taking a breath, Tavarra placed her hand to his lips and held down his chest with the other. His tongue stroked her flesh, sending a delicious shiver down her spine, as he sucked and drank deeply. When his teeth started to clamp down, she took her palm away again. Then she handed him the water beside him and he quietly took a few sips.

Perin's shoulders remained slumped, his expression grim. She couldn't keep telling him that it was okay—she needed to give him some sort of distraction. Perhaps she was playing with fire, but she didn't believe that he would attack her at that moment when she pressed her mouth to his soft lips.

It took him a second, but he kissed her in return, then snapped his head back a little, his chest heaving up and down. He didn't fully shift away from her, though.

"Did that help at all?" Tavarra asked, scanning his handsome face.

"I don't know."

"Don't be a fool and lie." She inched her face closer as he leaned in. This time she let her lips gently caress his, and he moved his against hers. Perin intertwined their fingers on her right side, and he softly rubbed the wrist on her other arm, careful to not touch where she had been hurt. However, the healing ointment was helping, and even if it wasn't, she wouldn't have minded right then.

While her lips sailed across his, and he drank hers in, Perin slid their joined hands to the back of his neck, then released them so her palm rested on his warm skin. His fingers trickled down the sides of her body until they gripped her waist and pulled her closer so that her legs straddled his hips. A heat ignited within her, drifting straight to her center.

Perin tilted his head forward, his hot breath brushing her ear as he whispered, "I don't know what the fuck I'm doing, or if I'm even doing this right."

She held back a laugh because he was doing everything right. "You're doing just fine."

As she started to move against him, his hands gripped tighter as they danced in the same rhythm. The speed picked up, making him groan, making her gasp, but he needed the escape more than she did.

"Do you want me to take care of you?" she murmured and pressed a kiss to the tip of his nose.

"You can do whatever you want." Perin bit his lower lip and tried to fight a smile. "You always do."

"Then lie back."

He finally listened. Tavarra shimmied his pants down just enough and pulled him out. Back at Lana's, she had seen him in full form while he was healing, but this was different—she *felt* different toward him.

His eyes remained closed while she stroked his length up and down and listened to his breathing increase. When she placed her lips around his thickness, Perin let out a low groan, and his hands came to her face and drifted to her hair.

Tavarra focused on him, but she couldn't help but relish in what she was doing, the flavor of him—it had been too long since she had been this intimate with anyone.

She could feel the pleasure building inside of him through his pulse. Perin's body jerked, deep sounds spilling from his lips, finding the release he needed—and she tasted *all* of him. His hands remained in her hair, their chests both heaving.

Heart pounding in her chest, she drew up his pants and lay beside him. "Feel better?"

"Much."

With a small smile, she scooted to her spot by the wall and sat watching him, his expression mirroring hers.

Sometime during the night, she had drifted to sleep. A jolt from the room woke her up and her gaze automatically found Perin, sitting up. His eyes were glazed over and he let out a growl, teeth bared before he shook his head and gripped the sides.

With a frustrated sound, his hands moved to his mouth and coughed something white into his palm. A tooth. "Fuck."

Tavarra took the tooth from his hand. "Open your mouth."

He did as she asked, and she peered inside. From the back, near the roof of his mouth, she could see where it had fallen from.

"I don't understand." She lowered her brows, staring at the tooth. "You've gone longer without eating before."

"In the stories, zombies eat the flesh of their own kind," he said, tracing the side of his jaw. "Maybe everything I've eaten besides the human man has only subsided the hunger or the aches, not the decaying."

"So you're saying you need another human..."

A loud splash came from outside the boat, causing it to lurch. Tavarra and Perin both toppled to the side.

They had made it to shore.

Twenty-Seven

Perin

"**I** will still offer you my arm," Vaden said when Perin exited the sand and stepped next to Tavarra at the edge of the forest.

"As tempting as that is," Perin answered sarcastically, "I must decline." The scent wafting up from the jovkin wasn't even affecting his hunger.

Perin's thoughts were elsewhere as he ran his tongue against the space where his tooth had fallen out. He couldn't help the anxious feeling flowing through him. When they had gotten off the boat, he'd expected the stranger who he'd feasted on to still be lying there, but someone from the man's village must have already scavenged the body and buried it.

"If you need me still," Vaden said to Tavarra, "just say the word."

"We'll be fine." Tavarra hadn't mentioned to the jovkin that Perin's tooth had fallen out, or he would most likely have changed his mind about leaving.

"You will find me past the stone mountains in a small hut," Vaden whispered. "Tell no one of the location."

Tavarra scrunched up her nose, and Perin frowned. Something felt strange about those words.

Vaden wrapped Tavarra's hand in between his and, with

his head, gave her a slight bow. "Because of you and this journey, I have learned to appreciate the things that are still here, and while I choose not to love again, I have come to love our friendship."

"As short as it's been." She smiled.

"The length of time matters not." He then turned toward Perin. "Do not harm her and take care of yourself."

Vaden gave a final goodbye and left them standing at the edge of the forest. But Perin couldn't focus on anything except the growing hunger in his belly.

Staring ahead, Perin knew the village wasn't too far, and he wanted to get away from it before the thing inside him chose to come out the way it had with the athers. "If we head east, the journey will take about two days if we move fast and only stop for one night."

"You can do it," Tavarra said.

Perin rubbed the tip of his tongue along his gum once more. He didn't know what else would fall off him along the way. "I'm going to be honest here. I don't know."

She tilted her head to the side. "We probably won't if we sit here and chat all day."

With a sigh, he started walking. He did what he could to shut out the aches and pains by paying attention to the sounds of the insects and the rustling of trees. Tavarra plucked a few pears and ate one as they passed the village.

Voices radiated from inside, and Perin did what he could to shut that out, too, because those sounds led to food that could fill what he desired at that moment the most.

As they passed the village, the sounds grew distant and he started to feel more comfortable with his surroundings. A twig snapped up ahead and his gaze jerked to where it had come from. Something in the wind whooshed. With quick actions, Perin pushed Tavarra out of the way right as an arrow zoomed past them. It would have penetrated her directly in the heart.

His chin lifted to the forest, and his heartbeat went up

several notches as soon as another arrow flew, but wasn't even close to hitting them. Lifting his sword, Perin slashed the flying object out of the way.

"Show yourself, coward," he bellowed, knowing exactly what tree the bastard stood behind.

A man with black hair and green eyes stepped out from behind the tree trunk, holding his bow with another arrow prepared to fly. "You stole one of our boats." His words came out slurred.

"Borrowed," Perin said with a shrug. "It's back now."

"It doesn't matter, she can't live." The man's eyes weren't ever focused on Perin—they had been on Tavarra, who stood frozen, glaring daggers at the bastard.

"Brice?" She said his name as though it were filth.

Perin's gaze shifted between Tavarra and Brice. Anger radiated off her as she tightened her fists, and his own fingers folded against his palm when he recognized the name. He wanted him dead. Especially after Brice had already made the first move by trying to kill Tavarra.

"Oh, sweet dweller"—Brice inched forward, stumbling—"no fangs any longer?"

Blood pumping, Perin raised his sword.

"Step any closer," Tavarra seethed, "and I'll rip you to shreds."

"You're lacking the claws now, too," Brice said, swaying, pointing at his scarred cheek. "And I'll break those fingers of yours before you can try."

He was going to die. Perin knew it, and he didn't give a fuck.

"Have you been drinking too much wine?" Tavarra asked, narrowing her eyes.

"You cost me my wife"—he ticked a finger up once, then twice—"and child. My daughter told my wife what she overheard between you and me in the forest."

"You only have yourself to blame for that," she said

without a care. "You're the one who deceived her."

Drunkenly, Brice dropped his arrow and notched another one. Perin pressed a hand to the bridge of his nose because he could slice this bastard's throat or stab him in the heart before he ever got his arrow to the string. It must have been luck that his first shot had been good aim.

Darting forward, Tavarra smacked the bow from Brice's hand. "Stop!"

Perin didn't want to interfere until he had to. If he had to. She'd want it this way. This was her fight, even though he wanted the bastard dead.

With her unhurt hand, Tavarra wrapped it around Brice's throat. He attempted to push her backward, but she was too strong for him. Movement came from Brice's side, and Perin saw him reach for his blade. She should have just snapped his neck.

That was the end of it. It was now his turn. Perin barreled forward and swung his blade, slicing off Brice's arm. In shock, Tavarra released Brice as his hand flew up to the wound. Perin peered down at the arm on the ground and Brice's horrified face as he let out a cry.

Despite knowing Brice was too weak to do anything now, Perin pressed his blade to the man's throat. "Just know that I could have easily killed you, but deep down, I know Tavarra doesn't want you dead, and that's the only reason I didn't stab you through your heart." Scowling, he pulled his sword back. "Go home."

As blood leaked from the wound, Brice could barely form a sentence. "This is all your fault, Tavarra." Gripping his wound, he stumbled away in the direction of the village.

"We better go," Perin said, "unless you want to strangle villagers today that will probably be coming our way if we stay here."

She covered her mouth and didn't say anything.

"I'm not going to apologize for what I just did. He was

going to kill you."

"No, it's not that." Tavarra walked forward and grabbed the arm on the ground. "Here. If Eza was around, I would tell her that I should have killed that bastard the last time we saw him. You were wrong, I would have been fine with him dead." She whirled around and headed east toward the Stone of Desire.

Perin followed her, inhaling the scent of the flesh. He knew he needed it, he wanted to eat—the aches in his stomach were pleading with him to. But he still hesitated until Tavarra turned her head over her shoulder and demanded, "Eat it."

He obeyed and lifted the arm to his nostrils, an unnatural growl escaping his lips, his eyes almost glazing over as he stared at the crimson peeking out from the end. Avoiding looking at Tavarra, Perin bit into the flesh, attempting to hold onto himself but losing the battle to the immaculate taste. Each bite better than the last.

When Perin finished, the aching in his stomach ceased, and he felt good, more than good. But he wasn't sure if it could last two more days.

Each step Perin took was one step closer to the unknown, to answers, to a possibility that could wind up being nothing. His heart beat furiously in his chest. They had stopped by a cave for the night, and Tavarra was building a fire for the drogwai that Perin had caught.

If he had to end up staying this thing he now was, then Rhona was better off thinking he was dead. He would keep away from her and Tavarra and come back to this cave or another place where he would let himself rot from the inside out until there was nothing left. That was the better option.

"Do you want to try some of the meat?" Tavarra asked

before placing it on the fire.

"No." The smell assaulted his nostrils, and he knew the flavor wouldn't satisfy him.

The night had gotten cooler inside the cave, and Perin held his hands over the fire, letting the warmth mold against his skin.

Once Tavarra finished eating, he peered down at her left hand. "How are your fingers?"

"They're already missing being whole, but the ointment is really helping."

Gently he grasped her wrist and brought her palm to his lips to press a kiss to the center. He ran his thumb softly against the skin at her wrist. "I'd kiss them if they were healed." His thoughts circled to the night before. Her kissing him, and not only on his mouth. He hadn't known if he'd been doing anything right, but *she* had done everything right.

"Soon enough, they will be." Her eyes met his. "So we should be there tomorrow? That means crossing a swamp again, and I'm really getting tired of walking through murky things."

"It's not so bad." His lips twitched, and he released her hand.

She quirked a brow and moved down to lay on her side.

"Okay, it's tedious, but at least there aren't hags in this one."

"I suppose." She smiled. "Goodnight."

"Goodnight." Perin lay down and studied the fire flames flickering, wondering if his father was somewhere in the afterlife or had he just vanished from existence. He hoped it was the latter. Closing his eyes, he watched the color behind his lids change from different versions of orange until he stopped thinking, and his breaths became even.

Sometime during the night Perin's eyes flew open. His bones felt as if the muscles had come unattached, as though every part of him had no real stability. The scent that lured him over and over on his journey hit his nostrils, stronger than ever. A low growl escaped his lips as his teeth clacked together. The pain became so raw that his eyes felt glassy. Two warm hands pressed against his cheeks—he snapped his teeth, but she didn't move her palms.

"Perin!" She shook his head.

It took him a few moments, but when she called his name again, the trance lifted.

"Focus," Tavarra said slowly.

"I can't." He sat up, shivering. "Everything inside me burns."

Tavarra stared at him for a moment, her brows lowered. "I don't think you should go to sleep. It seems to make things worse."

Something behind the scab in his stomach twitched, causing a flash of pain, and he let out a howl.

"This may be temporary, but we're doing it again because it seemed to at least help with the aches the last time." Tavarra made a narrow cut on her palm.

Perin shook his head, but she continued to hold it below his nostrils anyway. *This is the last time.* He brought her palm to his lips, and as before, the taste of her blood was salty with a flavor he couldn't begin to describe. The liquid flowed down his throat to the place that needed it the most. When he couldn't help but need more, his teeth clamped down and she ripped her hand away before he punctured her skin. She handed him his water, and he drank it, trying to forget how good she tasted.

The aches had mostly subsided, but still softly beat somewhere inside him, reminding him they could stir at any time. His eyes started to close.

"Don't go to sleep." Tavarra placed her hands to his cheeks again. "Kiss me."

"I don't think that's a good idea." He chuckled, fully alert then.

"Like last night, let me help you focus on something else."

"Of course I want to kiss you, but do you really want me like this?"

"We do what's necessary. And if I didn't, I wouldn't offer."

That was true. Tavarra didn't do anything she didn't want to.

Leaning forward, she pressed her lips to his, and he didn't hesitate as he had the previous night. Perin glided his lips against hers, caressing his tongue with hers, absorbing her warmth. He learned by feeling her movements, the way he had an opponent when sword fighting. Both were like a dance, a thrill, but this was undeniably better.

She grasped the collar of his shirt and pulled him down with her until he was settled between her legs. Perin didn't know what the fuck to do again, but when her hands came down to his hips, urging him to rock against her, he did. It felt natural and good, maybe too good for them both because she released a moan that could only be one of pleasure.

At that moment, he wanted her hands in his hair, along with his shoulder blades, down his spine, in the waistband of his pants, just anywhere, and everywhere, touching every inch of his skin, none of it being left unexplored. And he wanted to do the same to her. Tavarra's single touch made him forget what he was fighting.

He drew up her shirt a little to feel the spark of her warmth.

"Do you want to go further than last night?" she asked, her voice husky. "I'll stop whenever you want me to."

"I want you to show me everything." Perin tugged his shirt over his head, and her hands roamed against his scars, being careful to not brush against the scab at his middle. He shivered at the touch, and he wondered if the scars had never been there, would he have been able to feel her fingers even more?

His pants came away next, and he turned her over to straddle him while she still remained fully clothed. He hauled the shirt over her head, exposing her beautiful breasts. This time he didn't turn his head away from her naked form as she removed her pants. He ran a hand down the center of her chest—her heart beating as much as his—then over her breast, her nipple pebbling as he gently stroked.

"Are you really sure?" she asked. "I know you haven't…"

"I'm sure." The aches in his body dulled even more while his body focused on other things. He didn't only want this as a distraction. He wanted her.

Perin ran his hand between her legs, feeling things he'd never felt before and things he'd want to feel again. When she pressed herself down on him, they both gasped at the same time, and neither one moved as her gaze tangled with his, then the most glorious thing happened as she started to shift forward and back. She guided his hands to her hips, and she rocked faster, harder.

When Tavarra came—her gasps even beautiful—everything about her face relaxed from the euphoria. Each of her enticing movements, her soft fingers at his chest, had altered his hunger into a different form, growing more intense until he couldn't hold back and let out the release he needed.

She collapsed against his chest, and he rolled her to his side, not wanting to pull out of her just yet as both their chests inflated and deflated, sweat slicking their bodies. Then he finally did.

Neither one chose to sleep. They watched each other in a way that was new and different, that maybe could become even more one day. She would be fine without him and he would be fine without her. But he didn't want to just be fine. He wanted to be better. So for her and what could be, he would try to make it one more day.

Morning came, and they finally started to dress. Tavarra stopped him before he tossed on his shirt. "Wait."

"Yeah?" Perin asked.

"How come you kept your scars a secret so long from Rhona, yet you didn't try to hide them from me?"

"I don't know," he said, thinking about it. "But I probably would have if I hadn't been so delirious from the infection. Then after you saw them, I couldn't undo it anyhow." He paused and gave her a smirk, throwing his shirt over his head. "And you were comfortable to be around."

Tavarra rolled her eyes. "Even when I was angry?"

"Especially when you were angry."

Perin placed a soft kiss to her mouth, letting it linger for a split-second. "Last night was more than I could have asked for."

"It was amazing." She placed her hand against his cheek. "Now, let's get to the Stone."

After leaving the cave, they sprinted toward the Stone of Desire. The sooner he got there, the better. They skirted around trees, ducked under branches, watched the vast areas change into different colors as they entered new parts of the forest. The swamp neared, and Perin was about to give Tavarra a huge smile when he glanced down at his left hand. The fingernails on his pinky and ring finger had changed color to a light shade of gray. Both had lifted, and when he touched them, they broke right off.

Tavarra studied the nails on the ground in silence.

"Just cross," he said as a throb at his temple developed.

Perin stepped into the swamp, the thickness more like a barrier to slow him down. Gritting his teeth, he pushed through its texture as the suns beat down on him. Once he reached the other side, he pulled himself out and helped Tavarra. A hard throb came at his temple again. Something was going on with his head. As pain laced and radiated through his body, things started to become confusing.

Tavarra didn't even ask what was wrong—she took his hand and guided him the rest of the way. It had been so long since he'd been here that everything started to look similar, or maybe that was just because his sweat-covered body was growing achier with each movement.

As the pink then black leaves came into focus, he remembered them and knew they were getting closer. When Perin had left the Stone after Belen had sent him, he'd picked a few of those leaves and held them tightly before shredding them to pieces because the Stone hadn't helped him.

Up ahead, a white rock stood out like a lantern underneath a night sky with its rose-shaped top highlighted by the suns.

"We made it," Tavarra murmured.

Perin couldn't help but feel as though he were dreaming.

Twenty-Eight

Perin

Perin swayed in front of the Stone of Desire, drenched in sweat, starving, aching, his thoughts a jumbled mess. Tavarra stood beside him, her warm hand holding his clammy one, her scent smelling wonderful, blissfully so. He wanted to bask in it, he wanted to taste it, but he could control himself for a while longer. If this didn't work, he would ask her to leave, no matter how much he wanted her to stay.

"Come with me," Perin said.

"You can do it. I've done this before, remember?" Tavarra gave him a reassuring smile.

"I don't want to do it alone." And that was the truth.

"But you said, in the beginning, you wanted to." She laughed, her eyes glistening as she kissed his knuckles. He shook, eyes fluttering as he tried to control his inner demon. Even though part of him knew he didn't want to, Perin still yearned to rip her apart and taste what was inside. He bit his tongue to try to prevent himself from acting out because … he loved her.

He. *Loved.* Her. And he couldn't tell her that because he'd died once before, and he could very well still have a horrific ending now if the Stone of Desire didn't answer.

Taking the initiative, Tavarra dragged him forward and propped their entwined hands on top of the rose-shaped stone. Perin untangled their fingers and set his palm flat against the rough surface, her hand folding on top of his.

"Are you there?" Perin focused his attention directly on the Stone. "I've brought what you asked. Will you answer my desire?"

It answered almost immediately, letting his impatience wane away. The ground quaked roughly against his boots as it had the last time. He and Tavarra both moved backward at the same time, his fingers brushing hers. Perin didn't need her to be near him. He wanted her to be.

The alabaster rock peaked up from the ground, blooming toward the suns which shone down on the rose-shaped etching. A thunderous ruckus grew heavier as the Stone fully erupted.

"It likes to make an entrance, doesn't it?" Perin said, trying to sound light yet shattering on the inside.

"It really does." Tavarra nodded, her eyes not leaving the Stone.

From the rock body, two arms protruded, two legs slithered out, and its bald head poked forward. Marble black eyes appeared as the lids creaked upward. Then it crawled forward until it hovered directly above him, creating a darkened shadow.

"Where is it?" the voice boomed in his head, louder than ever.

Perin reached to Tavarra for the lavender liquid, then held it up high. "Right here."

Inside his head, a sound came that he was not expecting— it was something akin to a sigh of relief. Even that vibrated in his skull.

"Give it to me," the voice demanded, almost desperately.

Perin wasn't a fool. He pulled the bottle to his chest. "Do what you promised, then you can have it."

He expected the Stone to tell him to go fuck himself, but

instead, it brought a hand to the ground and held it open.

Perin didn't move. *He* wanted to tell the Stone to go fuck itself.

"I can hear all your thoughts." The Stone patted the ground again. "Come on, then."

Perin had a hard enough time trusting anyone, and he didn't trust this thing one bit. But with the growing hunger in his belly, he knew this was his only option. He shuffled forward and stepped onto the pale palm. Before he could ask what was going to happen next, the fingers closed around him, sucking away the color of the world.

There was darkness and not an ounce of light, and for a moment, he felt like the little boy he'd once been. The one who'd been scared of his father, the one who no longer was. That little boy was one who may have given up on himself at times but knew his sister would always survive. The way he knew he could survive now.

After who knows how much time passed, the fingers opened, letting the light filter back in.

He searched around, his eyes settling on Tavarra, and he smiled as soon as his feet touched the ground. What felt like an imaginary fist slammed into his stomach, and he clasped his abdomen as his knees buckled. Perin caught himself with one hand, while his knees smacked the ground. His stomach thumped with heavy pains, his joints screamed with murder, his insides felt as if they were being sliced to shreds with sharpened claws.

With everything he could, he held back his scream until he couldn't. The thump dulled until there was a new kind of pain, one so deep at his stomach that he couldn't catch his breath.

Tavarra crashed to her knees beside Perin and shouted, "What have you done to him?"

"He wanted to be happy," the Stone said. "So, I took away his curse."

"He's bleeding!" Tavarra screamed. "You bastard!"

Sure enough, when Perin glanced down, crimson coated his hands and tunic. He knew then with his whole heart what was happening. He was dying again. It had all been for nothing. But not nothing—he'd gotten to spend time with Tavarra and know his sister was all right.

"I love you," he whispered the words to her for the first time.

"Help him!" she shouted.

"Pour a drop of the liquid on the wound," the Stone answered.

Perin's hands were too weak to lift his shirt, but Tavarra was already pushing the tunic up. He could feel himself fading as he had before, when something as cold as ice hit his middle. Frozen daggers seemed to drag themselves inside his wound and tear him to pieces. Just when he thought he could never experience a harsher kind of pain in his life, he was dead wrong.

Then, as if it had never been there, it was gone.

He breathed heavily, in and out, in and out.

"Next time, do not speak so soon until things are finished being explained," the Stone bellowed.

Perin folded his arms across his stomach as if he were a child.

"Now, I must ask you for one favor," the Stone continued, pressing a hand to its chest. "I need you to pour two drops in since the bottle is so small."

"Where?" Perin asked. The creature had no mouth, no nose, no ears.

"My eyes. One in each."

Well, that answers my question.

The Stone shifted to its back, and Perin grabbed the bottle from Tavarra, her expression relieved and tinged with uncertainty. He then moved closer to the large head, and slowly climbed up until he was hunched on top of the face in between the eyes. With ease, he poured one drop in each eye.

As he climbed back down to the ground, it all felt absurd. What was the Stone doing? Why was it doing this? What was the point of everything?

The Stone started to convulse, shaking violently after Perin hopped to the ground. Tavarra yanked him back by the collar of his shirt as one of the arms crashed down where he'd been, dust rising upward.

"What is going on?" Tavarra asked the same question he'd been thinking.

"I think that maybe we shouldn't have retrieved the lavender." Something was wrong.

"Then you would be a monster or dead, you fool!"

Neither one made a move to run, but he and Tavarra were both smart enough to unsheathe their swords. In front of his very eyes, the Stone decreased in size, shrinking smaller and smaller until it was maybe the size of Rhona. Dark hair sprouted from the skull as the skin changed from alabaster to a rich olive. Fingernails, nose, ears, lips, breasts—it all appeared. And then the eyelids covered in thick lashes opened to irises of a deep lavender.

Perin had no words.

Tavarra had no words.

The Stone had no words—this *woman*.

The woman pushed herself up and murmured, "Thank you."

"Who are you?" Perin asked, his jaw hanging open.

"Zada."

"The Goddess?" Tavarra's eyes widened.

"I'm almost free," Zada replied. "I've been living this immortal life for hundreds and hundreds of years, connected to different worlds, unable to do anything, or say anything to anyone living, only answer desires. But Perin wasn't completely alive, and he needed the liquid for me to answer his wish, and it was the only thing that could cure me. However, I was unable to mention that directly. Now he can have a chance at being happy.”

“We need to get you some clothing,” Tavarra rushed the words out.

Perin’s shirt was filthy, but he started to tug it off.

“There’s no time for that,” Zada began. “I didn’t foresee this part. I knew you’d be happy, Tavarra, but I didn’t realize Perin would play a part in that.”

Out of nowhere, a sharp cry came from Zada. She pressed a hand against her chest. “My immortality here has ended since my curse is broken. I can now go home.” She started to fall backward. Perin shot forward to scoop her up before her body crashed to the ground. When her body connected with him, it turned to dirt in his arms. He vainly tried to hold what was left of her body, standing up, but it all cascaded back to the earth, becoming part of it.

For the first time in his life, Perin didn’t know what to do—didn’t know whether to keep holding onto the dirt or whether to move away.

Tavarra’s trembling hand clasped his shoulder. “It’s okay. She’s free. You’re free. I’m free. No more desires, no more wishes, just choosing to live. Just as I choose to love you.”

Perin’s chest swelled at her words, and he knew he could do it all. “I choose to do the same.” He placed his arms by his side, the remainder of the dirt sprinkling into the ground.

“Now, are you ready to see your sister? I think you’ve kept this hidden long enough.”

The journey to Quil’s village, or Rhona’s, was different. *He* felt different. Perin wondered what it would be like not having to worry any longer. Yes, there would still be threats while hunting, but there wasn’t the fear of transitioning into something else, not for him, not for Tavarra. They were now who they were always meant to be.

Once they arrived at the village, music filled the air. There were people working, children gathering fruit or playing, others learning through books.

He didn't stop to talk to anyone, that just wasn't him. Or Tavarra. Lana's wide porch came into view, her potted plants in full bloom with yellow and white flowers. He picked a white flower to give to his sister—might as well have something while asking for her forgiveness. Again. Then he plucked a yellow one and handed it to Tavarra.

"You know you just picked Lana's flowers."

"She can grow more." He grasped it from Tavarra's fingers and tucked it into her hair behind her ear.

Tavarra knocked on the door, and they waited as the wind blew around them. No one answered.

"She must not be home," he said. "We can try Quil's."

No one answered that door, either. Perin's fingers twitched with impatience. What if they were still gone on their journey? Then he heard it. The clinking of swords from the back of the house.

Perin darted around to the side of the house, then slowed down. He gripped the flower stem as he peered around the corner. Rhona swung her sword at Quil, and he blocked it. His sister appeared the same, except her blonde curls had grown a little longer, wilder, while Quil's dark locks had been cut. His chest swelled with happiness, and he couldn't be more proud of her.

Quil was a little less pitiful, but she still knocked him onto his back. Laughing, Lana shook her head and signed something to Quil. Rolling his eyes and smiling, he signed back. Another woman chuckled—Lana's partner, Emma, reclined against a tree.

Rubbing his jaw, Perin thought that maybe he shouldn't interrupt. They were all smiling and happy and would be fine without him. He turned around.

Tavarra placed a hand to his chest, holding him back with her strength. "They'll be even happier when they see you."

"Maybe it's better this way."

"There you go again, choosing for people." Tavarra narrowed her eyes. "Let Rhona see you before you make a decision."

Footsteps beat against the ground, rushing toward them. He whirled around, finding Rhona coming at him with a sword.

Perin didn't think, he unsheathed his right in the nick of time as hers clashed against his. And she knocked him to the ground.

"What is this?" Rhona's sword didn't move from his neck, digging in harder. "It can't be possible. What have *you* done?" Her voice was tinged with fear.

Tavarra looked as though she wasn't prepared for this reaction. "I didn't do anything."

Perin smiled then. "You won."

His sister's sword fell from her grasp, and she backed up with her hand covering her mouth. Quil came up beside her, lost for words.

Lana signed to Quil and said, "It's true. He's alive. He had me wait to tell you the story and vanished on me before I could go with him."

"*What*?" Rhona shrieked.

"You didn't even tell me?" Emma's auburn brows went up.

Perin stood and brushed the dirt from his pants. "Let me explain, sister." He told her the story from the beginning, about how he'd woken up, gone across the sea before coming back to the Stone of Desire, and how it had ended.

"Oh," he added, "the jovkin who came with us is descended from Junah. Remember the story?"

"I don't care about any stories right now!" Tears streaked Rhona's cheeks as she hurled herself forward and wrapped her arms around him.

Letting out a breath, he returned his sister's hug. "I missed you." He pulled back and placed the white flower in her hair. "Sorry I didn't have a better gift."

"If only I had been here to go with you…"

"Then maybe things wouldn't have ended up as they have." Perin smirked. "And the only reason you did win just now was because you caught me off guard, sister."

"Excuses, excuses."

"How about you show me my new home." His smile widened to a full one as he looked from Rhona and settled it on Tavarra.

"Is that a real smile I see?" Rhona asked, tears continuing to fall.

"Maybe it is."

Epilogue

Tavarra

"**D**o you think he'll still be there?" Tavarra asked, blocking the sun with her hand and gazing back at the stone mountains that she and Perin just walked through.

"From what I know of Vaden, it seemed like it was the right place for him to be, so we can only go there and see." Perin shrugged, biting into a plum.

Tavarra rubbed her eyes, still exhausted from the night before. They had stopped to camp for the night in one of the caves in the mountains. Neither one of them had gotten much sleep with Tavarra teaching his body new things, and him exploring hers in creative ways.

Placing a hand to Perin's chest, she pressed her mouth against his when he lowered his plum, tasting the sweet flavor of fruit lingering on his lips. "I'm glad you didn't die." When she thought he was dying the second time at the Stone of Desire, she had almost lost her ability to breathe.

"You would have been fine," he said, pushing one of her locks of hair behind her ear that had fallen.

"As time passed, I would have survived, but this is a much better option." Tavarra didn't want to think about the other option. Even now, she didn't know what would happen tomorrow—there was only today.

Perin adjusted his sword, not meeting her gaze. "Does that mean you'll stay with me in the village?"

"Perhaps." Her lips twitched.

In a flash, Perin tipped her backward and softly caressed his lips against hers, his hand lingering near the skin at her spine where her tunic had risen, heating up her body.

"If this is how you intend to persuade me, I suppose I will." She laughed and pulled the plum from his hand and took a bite after he stood her back up.

There was one more hill they needed to go up, and somewhere below was where Vaden had said he would be. Tavarra and Perin shared the rest of the plum as they trudged up the hill, then came to a stop on top beside two trees without any leaves. Up ahead and down below, there sat a valley, open and vast. In the center rested a lone shelter, poorly built with sticks and leaves clustered together. She was surprised the wind hadn't knocked it down, but it must be stronger than it appeared.

Tavarra wandered down the hill first, then came to a stop in front of the shelter with Perin. Before she could knock, the door flew open and out stepped Vaden with a smile, his golden eyes bright.

"I thought I heard something out here." He leaned over and wrapped his arms around her. She enfolded hers to his back and rested her head against his shoulder. Vaden released her and pulled Perin in for a hug, except Perin's arms remained by his sides, his expression slightly uneasy, until he gave Vaden a little pat on his back.

"Now tell me why you're way out here," Tavarra started, "and why you told me you had nowhere to go when we first met."

Vaden's eyes flickered with amusement, and he ran a hand against one of his horns. "I wanted to show you this in person, and I trust you, but I also trust them. I made a promise to keep their secret safe. I've already told them you have a story they would want to hear."

"*They?*" Perin asked, his jaw grinding back and forth.

"*Them?*" Tavarra didn't see anyone else outdoors besides Vaden—whoever he was talking about had to be inside the rickety shelter. Her shoulders tensed.

Vaden walked to the corner of the shelter, where he snatched a grassy mat away that blended in with the ground. Tavarra and Perin shuffled forward to where a hole rested. They both leaned over and peered down it.

Before Tavarra could say anything, Vaden cupped his mouth and called down the hole, "It's safe now."

In an explosion of cacophony, a beating and swooshing noise came from below, like that of the tiny dragons. Tavarra pulled Perin back and expected to see the colorful dragons come out. But no, she was incredibly wrong. Dark glossy wings and pale bodies came into view, and she gasped, pressing a hand to her mouth.

Bats. They were bats. Not one, not two, but hundreds and hundreds of bats. Each one reminded her of Eza, fairy-like, but darker and sweeter versions. The faces of the creatures were all different—round, thin, heart-shaped, or oval. Yet, the wings, the pointy ears, the sharp teeth were just like Eza's— her friend.

Tears slid down her cheeks, both happy and sad because all this time, the bats had been hidden underground. Eza could have come here if only they had known. Eza *wasn't* the last of her kind and Tavarra knew her friend would have been proud.

"Hey, this is supposed to be a happy time," Vaden said after she forgot he was there.

"I *am* happy, very happy."

The bats danced and flew around the three of them before shooting back into their underground cave.

"They actually prefer it down there." Vaden placed the grassy mat back in its place. "They've adjusted to their own world below ground over the years."

"Can we bring my sister here?" Perin asked. "The one I told you was descended from Bray."

"I think they would actually love that," Vaden said. "You can ask them before you two leave and after you tell them your stories. But first, how about coming inside, and I will tell you the tale of how I came across them. Or should I say … Aubrey did, and how we promised together to always keep them safe." He paused with a sad smile. "This is where we lived."

Tavarra knew at that moment the real reason he hadn't gone back sooner was because this place reminded him so much of Aubrey.

Perin placed his hand into hers, intertwining their fingers. "Where to, after this?"

"We'll go home and get Rhona." Tavarra didn't think she would ever find something that she thought of as home again. Homes weren't always a permanent place to expand across someone's life, sometimes they were temporary, but there was always a lasting place for them in one's heart. Eza was still Tavarra's home, but so was Perin, and so was Laith.

Did you enjoy Shadowed By Despair?

Authors always appreciate reviews, whether long or short.

Subscribe to Candace's Awesome Newsletter for the latest news and giveaways!

Join Candace's Facebook Group: Candace's Pretty Monsters

Turn the page for Brenik's bonus short story!

SURROUNDED

BY

LIGHT

Brenik

After all this time, Brenik still loved her.

Love was a devastating thing.

And for someone he had known for only a short while, Rana lingered in his thoughts, despite how much time had passed. Minutes, hours, weeks, months, years, eons? Whatever it was, it had been too much time.

Brenik had died. He destroyed himself to save his sister—Brayora. Wasted time. That was what his life had been. He had wasted it being envious of Bray, and in the end, he missed her so much.

There was a bond that still connected him to her, and he knew in his heart that she had searched for him. But in this afterlife, he remained hidden, and wanted it to stay that way.

She was probably out there somewhere happy with Wes. Fucking Wes. Brenik still hated that prick. But when Brenik had first come to the afterlife, he heard whispers. He had been able to save the kid by telling Bray to rush him to the Stone of Desire. Luca was always meant to be the savior, and even though Brenik's actions led to the kid's original death, he came back and did what was destined all along. Luca had saved as many humans as he could by helping them cross into Laith from a dying Earth. Too bad Luca couldn't have saved Brenik's soul.

Yet, he hadn't ended up in a hell of eternal flames. Instead he ended up in the hell of his own fucking mind.

Go find her, he thought. *Her. Her. Her. Rana. Haven't you waited long enough?*

"No," Brenik whispered aloud to no one but his damn self. He pressed his back against the cave wall and propped his arms on his knees. There was nothing in this cave for him to see—he chose to keep it dark, and let the blackness surround him. But there was always the light at the opening, trying to beckon him forward.

He always chose to stay.

When he had woken in the afterlife, Brenik hadn't returned to his bat form as he had thought he would. The wings were gone and he was still almost human. He was still young. Just as he had wanted… An immortal life of being young, beautiful, flawless. And alone.

There was no hunger. No yearning for the taste of blood. That was all replaced with a different yearning, one that involved finding a woman who had changed everything. But Brenik couldn't. He had murdered her while making love to her. That was as unforgivable as it could get. It hadn't been intentional, but did that make it any better?

A screech clawed at his ears as something plopped to the floor of the cave. Brenik leaped up and peered at a tiny glowing light. The white light grew brighter and brighter. He closed his eyes and when he opened them back up, the cave was illuminated. Not a touch of darkness enveloped him … or the small thing on the floor…

"Ow!" A high-pitched voice reverberated off the walls.

He knelt toward the pale object and froze, taking a deep swallow. His gaze settled on obsidian wings with protruding veins, unfurling from a pale back. For a moment, he had thought it was his sister Bray—wished it was—but the bat wasn't her. Two black braids draped over the female's shoulders, and a violet dress without sleeves hit right above her knees. Her big gray eyes peered up at him.

Astonishment turned to raw anger as his heart pounded and the blood in his veins heated. "You need to leave."

"Who are you?" the bat asked as she stood and brushed the

dust off her dress and wings.

He didn't know anymore. Every day was the same, and he just blended into his dark surroundings. "No one."

She placed her hands on her hips and cocked her head. "*No one* has to have a name. Unless you need me to give you one? How about Orja?"

What the fuck? Maybe this was Hell… "I don't need a name. Now leave."

"Only if you tell me your name first."

He sighed. "Brenik."

The bat gasped, flapping her wings and spinning in the air until she was balancing across from him. "I'm Eza."

Narrowing his eyes, he stayed silent. He didn't care what her name was. And the more he talked to her, the more he would tarnish her, like he had everyone else.

"No, I know you!" She tapped his nose. "I know one of your descendants, or at least Bray's descendant. Her name is Rhona. And I think you and I are related."

He took a step away from her until his back struck the wall. An emotion washed over him and he had to push it away by taking a hard swallow. "I don't give a fuck." But in reality, he really did.

"You already remind me of my other friend Perin."

Curiosity got the better of him, the way it used to get Bray. "Where is this descendant now?"

"Oh, she's still alive in Laith." Eza then ran a hand across her throat, her expression turning grim for a moment. "I died and it wasn't a good death. Jovkins are a dangerous thing … and bitey."

Memories flooded his mind. A jovkin named Junah had raised him with his sister before he and Bray escaped Laith. At times, he hadn't treated Junah the way he should have, but there was nothing he could do about that now. She was probably in peace with Bray somewhere here, too.

"I knew a good jovkin once." He thumped the back of his

head against the wall and slid down to sit on the floor. The room was still bright, almost blinding. It had been so long since he had seen light like this.

The bat seemed to search around the room, studying the ceiling, the pebbled ground, the jagged walls. "Why are you sitting here alone?"

He sucked in a sharp breath and stared at his hands. "I deserve it. For everything I did."

"It can't be that bad."

This female was too trusting. She didn't know him at all. "I *killed* humans and was cursed."

"One of my friends killed all sorts of creatures including humans"—she shrugged—"and Tavarra's not bad." Her gaze lingered on him as though in challenge.

He arched a brow. "Are you sure about that?"

"She's cursed… Not by choice."

The Stone of Desire. He remembered it asking him to choose, and he had. "I was cursed as well. But I was responsible for my own path. I was selfish."

"Do you regret the decision?"

He didn't have to think about his answer because it would always be the same. "Yes."

"Then I think you've been in here long enough." Eza flew closer to him again. "You do know that hundreds and hundreds of years have passed since you died? I think that's enough, isn't it?"

So, it *had* been a long while since he had died. It didn't change anything. "No."

"I can search for my family later." She steepled her fingers together. "I think you need the company."

The old Brenik would have wanted to shove her out of the cave so she could go somewhere else, but he was too tired. And he hated to admit it, but after all this time, the company wasn't so bad.

"Eza, I loved a woman once," he whispered.

"Then why are you here?" The bat's fingers dug into his shoulder. "Find her."

And what would he even say if he found Rana again? "I killed her. Unintentionally."

"All can be forgiven."

He didn't believe that. Not for a moment. Some might be good at forgiveness, but he wasn't. "Would you forgive the jovkin who killed you?"

"If she was sorry enough, I would. But it's in their nature to do the things they do. Was it in yours?"

Envious and selfish had always been two words to describe him perfectly. But he had never been capable of murder. Not until he had become almost human. "Only because of the curse."

"Then let me help you find her."

"Why are you so worried about this?" Brenik leaned his head against the wall and closed his eyes.

Her light frame dropped down on his shoulder and his body stilled. Brenik opened his lids and stared at the bat, curled up on him, her wings tightly woven around her. She was already asleep, most likely exhausted from her journey after death. He remembered being tired when he had first arrived, too.

Brenik was still tired. Tired of this hell he had put himself in. As he closed his eyes, all he could think about was how Bray loved the *Peter Pan* story. In that moment, Eza reminded him of Tinker Bell, which would make him Peter fucking Pan. And it must have been exactly what Luca had thought when he was with Bray. Brenik hated that damn story. It was about some little shit who lured children to a shitty land where they never grew up. Who the hell would want that? Only an idiot. But Brenik had made the most idiotic decision of all.

Blowing out a breath, he closed his eyes once more, and for the millionth time, thought about how he could have, would have, done things differently. Yet the past couldn't be changed, only the present could alter the future. And sitting here, in this cave, would make it so that everyone remained okay.

Something hard jabbed Brenik's face and he jerked awake. Two small hands were pushing at his cheek.

"Stop that!" he spat, wiggling his shoulder for Eza to dart off. But she didn't.

"I have a proposition for you," she chirped.

"I don't want to hear it."

"Oh, but you do. You're getting out of this cave and going to your love, and you will apologize."

Running a hand down his face, he stood with a sigh. "Listen, you may have come from Laith where people kill like nothing. But Earth wasn't like that. You get locked away for doing what I did."

"Look, you need to try," Eza huffed. "If she doesn't forgive you, then you can return here and I'll come with you."

Brenik stared hard at her. He may not have minded her company at the moment, but he didn't want her to sulk with him in the darkness for all eternity.

"Or I can just continue staying here now."

Dear God. He had never met someone so stubborn. Bray could be bad, but not like this. He could go with Eza for now, then ditch her if need be and find somewhere else to remain.

"Fine."

The bat didn't fly from his shoulder as he stood, only crossed her legs at the ankles and swung them against him.

The light seemed to call him when he drew closer to its magnetic pull. That was why he always remained at the back of the cave, away from any goodness.

As he slipped out of the opening, a world full of color enveloped him. He was completely surrounded by a rainbow of bright hues, and all he wanted was to say fuck this and go back into his cave. But his heart beat faster, his nerves soaring.

"Are you all right?" Eza asked, looking down at his unmoving feet. "Do you know where to go?"

"I know exactly where she is," he whispered. "I can choose to feel her if I want to. I can feel anyone." Just as anyone who truly wanted to search him out could have done. But he had shut off his aura so no one could easily find him. Not anymore, though. He knew it was reigniting. If anyone wanted to search him out, they would be able to now.

Fields of blue and red tulips, and white and pink flowering trees, covered the entirety of the afterlife. Above them, the sky was made of interweaving branches and purple and yellow petals.

As Brenik crossed through the flowers, spotted butterflies flew up and darted to another area of winding orange hills. So much brightness. But the world wasn't daunting—it was beautiful, lighting up the darkness within him.

He chose to walk then. Not turn around. Brenik walked and walked for what felt like days. He didn't sleep, didn't need to eat. Eza chatted to him about Laith, about her loved ones. He found himself not hating how she poured out her world to him. Maybe they *were* related somewhere down the line.

And then, at long last, there she was.

In the distance, standing beneath a tree raining bright ivory petals, she faced away from him. Even though so much time had passed, he couldn't deny that it was indeed her.

Dark hair fell to Rana's shoulders, brushing her warm brown skin. She wore a strapless pale-yellow dress that came to her ankles, and her feet were bare.

Was she alone in this afterlife? He was certain she had found someone else. Why wouldn't she have? Why would she wait around for someone who had lied and ended her life?

"Don't stop," Eza said softly. "That's her, right?"

Brenik clenched his fists, trying to make himself go

forward. He drew closer and closer, a gust of wind ruffling his hair, until he stood directly behind her. Maybe too close for the time they had been apart, but he didn't care.

A light scent struck his nostrils, and he inhaled her. She smelled the same, like spearmint. And this time, he didn't have to worry about hurting her.

"I wondered when you would crawl out of that cave." Rana whirled around on him, her dark eyes burning bright. Besides the length of her hair, she looked just as she had the last he had seen her, when they had kissed, when they had made love, when he had *killed* her.

So, she had known where he was. This entire time. "I'm sorry."

"Sorry for which part?" Rana cocked her head, and his eyes drifted to the mole under her lower lip. "Murdering me, not telling me the truth, or hiding away?"

"I'll give you space," Eza whispered near his ear. "Just keep talking. It's not going so bad." She took off and Rana watched the bat, but didn't ask who she was.

Brenik focused on Rana, inching closer. She probably needed space but he wasn't always good at doing what people needed. But he forced himself to take a step back and not cower. "All of it. What would you have done if I had told you?"

"I would have been frightened," she said.

"And then not talked to me."

"No." Rana clenched her jaw and crossed her arms, a few petals falling and sticking to her hair. "I would have eventually calmed down and then tried to help you."

Fuck giving her space. Brenik shifted forward, hoping she wouldn't back up. He placed his hand on her waist and drew her closer, then rested his head in the crook of her neck. His body trembled as tears came, ones that wouldn't stay tucked away, then he let himself sob. Sobbed like a child. He expected her to run, hoped she would run, and give him what he deserved.

Instead, Rana's arms folded around him and neither said anything as his body shook. Even after the tears stopped, even after his thoughts calmed, his body wouldn't stop shaking. She was comforting him, when she should have slapped him across the face and left him alone.

"I love you," he murmured against her shoulder. "I knew it from the moment I saw you in that bar."

Rana's body did move then and she tilted his head so he couldn't avoid looking anywhere else but at her. "You need to forgive yourself, Brenik. Someone else has been waiting for you, and you need to see her." With a gentle smile, she pointed behind him.

Brenik turned around and spotted a female with bright blue eyes and jet-black hair pulled into a single braid, appearing just the same. Bray. His sister. And she wasn't alone—Eza rested on her shoulder.

"Fuck." His breaths came out uneven. He couldn't do this. Couldn't. Couldn't. Couldn't.

"Forgive yourself, talk to your sister, then come back to me."

Brenik didn't want to leave Rana. There was the fear that she would disappear, and he would never find her again. He had wanted to stay hidden from her, but now that she was here, that he was seeing her, he didn't want her to leave. "Have you forgiven me?"

She blinked as though not wanting to give him an answer just yet. "I've had hundreds of years to do so. What do you think?"

He couldn't help but smirk. "I don't know. I've had hundreds of years to forgive myself and haven't."

"You've still got that old Brenik in there, but I feel there's much more to him now. Isn't there?"

Maybe she was right. There had been years and years for him to think, to change, to grow, and perhaps he had.

"I'll talk to Bray for now." He paused, not touching her yet wanting desperately to. "But are you with another?"

"I haven't been celibate, if that's what you're asking," she said, her expression not telling him anything else.

"I understand." Brenik could hear the sadness in his own words, and that was fine because he didn't want to hide that from her either.

"However, I'm not attached to anyone now." A warm smile played across her lips. "Someone always seems to linger in my head."

The way she did in his. "Can I kiss you?" It was too early, too impulsive to ask, but again, he couldn't bring himself to care.

In answer, she pressed her lips to his, soft and gentle, and he could feel it then. That spark between them. The one that had never left, no matter the hurt he had caused. Envy had destroyed so much of him, but it had been gone since the day he chose to save his sister. And in that cave, what he didn't know, was that he had been mending himself while trying to mend everyone else.

"We have all the time in the world to relearn each other," she whispered in his ear.

His fingers ran up the length of her spine, wanting to relearn every inch of her right then, but he knew not to rush it. He would take things slowly this time. No matter how torturous.

As he turned around, he murmured to the world surrounding him, "I forgive myself."

Brenik stepped toward his sister, pulling himself together. Eza jolted off Bray's shoulder, and his sister ran toward him with the biggest smile on her face. His lips curved up on one side when her arms flew around him.

"I've missed you, little brother." She beamed, out of breath.

"Don't worry, I'm still an asshole, but *I* will do better this time.”

Bray was just as perfect as she always was. Kind and sweet, and he didn’t feel the least bit envious of her.

“Come on, everyone wants to see you.” She tugged his hand, but he remained planted in place. Brenik glanced back over his shoulder one more time at Rana’s face.

“I’ll meet you back here tomorrow,” she called, tugging the loose petals from her hair.

Biting his lip, he asked, “Do you think you could love me too?”

“With your charm, anything’s possible.” Rana grinned.

That was good enough. It was something he could work with.

Brenik cradled Bray’s shoulders and drew her closer, letting her guide him through the flowering trees as she talked about Wes and Luca. And somehow, he controlled himself from calling Wes a prick. It was progress.

Second chance. That was what this would be. No lies. Only truths. And he would make sure the light would always overpower the dark.

Also From Candace Robinson

Wicked Souls Duology
Vault of Glass
Bride of Glass

Marked by Magic Duology
The Bone Valley
Merciless Stars

Cruel Curses Trilogy
Clouded By Envy
Veiled By Desire
Shadowed By Despair

Faeries of Oz Series
Lion (Short Story Prequel)
Tin
Crow
Ozma
Tik-Tok

Cursed Hearts Duology
Lyrics & Curses
Music & Mirrors

Immortal Letters Duology
Dearest Clementine: Dark and Romantic Monstrous Tales
Dearest Dorin: A Romantic Ghostly Tale

Campfire Fantasy Tales Series
Lullaby of Flames
A Layer Hidden
The Celebration Game
Mirror, Mirror

These Vicious Thorns: Tales of The Lovely Grim
Between the Quiet
Hearts Are Like Balloons
Bacon Pie
Avocado Bliss

Vampires in Wonderland Series
Rav (Short Story Prequel)
Maddie
Chess
Knave

Acknowlegments

Thank you to the readers who have been on this journey along with me! I can't thank you enough. I knew when I finished Veiled By Desire that Perin's story wasn't finished yet!

I'd like to thank my editors Live, Jackie, and Megan. Thank you so much for helping make this story better! Hannah, this cover you created for Shadowed is absolutely beautiful!

To Alexa, Donna, Amber H., Amber D., Vic, Patricia, and Gerardo, without you guys, I would curl in a ball somewhere!

Nate and Arwen, you two are the reason I breathe! Mom, you are what keeps me motivated!

And also to all those zombie movies I loved and adored and knew that deep down that there was still a bit of human left in there!

About the Author

Candace Robinson spends her days consumed by words and hoping to one day find her own DeLorean time machine. Her life consists of avoiding migraines, admiring Bonsai trees, watching classic movies, and living with her husband and daughter in Texas—where it can be forty degrees one day and eighty the next.

Connect with Candace:

Website: https://authorcandacerobinson.wordpress.com/
Facebook: https://www.facebook.com/literarydust
Twitter: https://twitter.com/literarydust
Instagram:
https://www.instagram.com/candacerobinsonbooks/
Goodreads:
https://www.goodreads.com/author/show/16541001.Candace
_Robinson